BEYOND CONNECTIONS

A Heart-Warming Collection of
FAMILY and RELATIONSHIP
Short Stories

All Stories Written by

LYNN MICLEA

BEYOND CONNECTIONS

A Heart-Warming Collection of
FAMILY and RELATIONSHIP
Short Stories
Written by Lynn Miclea

***

Other Short Story Collections by Lynn Miclea:

- *Beyond the Abyss* – Science Fiction
- *Beyond Terror* – Thrillers, Horror, and Suspense
- *Beyond Love* – Love and Romance
- *Beyond Connections* – Family and Relationships

ISBN: 979-8359324786
Independently Published

Cover photo from Pixabay.com

DEDICATION

This book is humbly dedicated to friends, family, and all my readers and supporters throughout the years who have believed in me, supported me, loved my stories, and given me encouragement when I needed it most.

And to my husband, Dumitru, for his patience, love, and undying support as I spent all my free time working on my books, struggling to find my way and make it all work.

Thank you all. Your support is very appreciated.

FOREWORD

Family, relationships, and close connections with others are vitally important, and they are necessary for our wellbeing and full enjoyment of life. Our connections with family and others color our entire world and affect who we are.

We all yearn for a personal closeness and intimacy with friends, family, and with someone special. Exploring these connections and relationships can open many different realms and touch us deep in our heart, bringing more meaning and fulfillment to our lives.

These connections, and the stories in this book, include parents and children, siblings, friends, adoption, abuse, discovering your own identity, learning to love yourself, dementia, grief and loss, finding love, and many more facets of family, relationships, and love.

I sincerely hope this collection of family and relationship short stories does all that for you and much more.

Sit back, relax, and enjoy these touching, enchanting, and heart-grabbing stories.

Thank you for stepping into *Beyond Connections*.

— *Lynn Miclea*
Author

TABLE OF CONTENTS

GOLD BUTTERFLY

Katy lay on her side in the bed, breathing deeply, pretending to be asleep. Desperation clawed at her. She needed to get out. Tonight was the night.

She heard Joel's footsteps approach, and she sensed him at the side of the bed checking on her. She kept her breathing deep and regular.

Apparently satisfied, Joel headed to the bathroom.

Katy didn't move. It could be a test. If he thought she was pretending, he would make sure it was impossible to leave. She would never get out. If he got angry, he might not even let her live.

She heard the shower being turned on. Still, she didn't move.

Finally, she heard the shower door close. She opened one eye. Nothing.

Pushing herself up slowly, she glanced around. The bathroom door was closed.

Now was probably the best chance she would ever have.

Trembling, her heart pounding in her chest, she got up, dressed as quickly as she could, and ran downstairs. She would only have a few minutes. This was the first time she had seen Joel leave the door key on the kitchen counter. He was usually not that careless, always keeping the key carefully hidden. Until tonight. And if she were caught, he would never be that careless again.

Taking the key, she carefully unlocked the cabin door, stepped out into the cold night air, and then closed the door quietly behind her. She held her breath and listened. She could still hear the shower in the bathroom upstairs.

Terrified and unsure, she froze for a few seconds, and then she ran.

Surrounded by trees, deep in the woods, she did not know which way to go. Having been brought there blindfolded a week earlier, she had no idea where she was. Joel had driven her to this area and then walked her along a dirt path to the cabin before removing the blindfold. She did not know where his car was or which way was the way out. She just knew she had to keep moving, and hopefully she would find a road or someone who could help.

Although it was hard to see in the dark, she rushed forward. A small amount of light from the half-moon filtered through the canopy of leaves above, but not much reached the ground. A few times, she tripped on roots or rocks in the dirt, but she caught herself and continued. She desperately needed to get far enough away that he wouldn't find her. She hoped that was possible.

She knew without a doubt Joel would come looking for her once he found her gone. And if he found her, he would be enraged and would very likely kill her. Memories of his abuse over the past few days nudged at her mind, but she quickly pushed them aside. She had to stay focused.

After running and stumbling a few times, she stopped to catch her breath for a few minutes. Her fingers absently checked her pocket. Was it still there? Her fingers closed around a small gold butterfly, given to her by her Aunt May before she died. "Always believe in yourself," her aunt had told her. "You are stronger than you think and you know what's right for you." Her aunt had placed the gold butterfly in her hand and closed her fingers around it. "I believe in you," she had said. "You need to believe in you, too."

Katy blinked back tears at the memory. She hoped the gold butterfly would give her strength and help keep her safe.

She resumed walking, being more careful now. A short time later, she heard a shout. Joel's voice. "Katy? Where are you?" She gasped and then tried to calm down. She stayed still and silent. "I'm gonna find you, Katy. You won't get away. You know that, right?"

She knew she had to move discreetly and quietly. She took a few steps and a twig under her foot snapped. She froze in place and listened. It did not seem like he heard it.

"Katy? Come on, you won't survive out here at night. You're gonna regret this. Where are you?"

His voice sounded farther away. Or maybe it was just her fear and she wasn't hearing well. She was not sure. She waited a few minutes. After not hearing anything more, she continued walking, going slower and being more cautious.

After what seemed like a couple hours, she shivered, the cold air settling deeper into her. She rubbed her arms, trying to get warmer. Would she survive a night out in the cold? Where would she find shelter? There was no safety in the woods, and the night was definitely getting colder.

She kept moving. She wished someone could help her. But no one knew she was gone or where she was, so no one would even be looking for her.

She knew she had briefly mentioned to her friend Jennifer that she was seeing Joel this weekend and that she was not happy with how he was treating her and was considering breaking up with him. But she did not speak to her friend every day, so Jennifer might not even realize she was missing. And even if she did, she wouldn't know where she had been taken. Katy didn't even know where she was herself. She clearly was on her own.

Needing to warm up, she rubbed her arms again. She had no idea Joel was capable of anything like this. And she had no idea what to do. A sense of hopelessness settled in her chest and she wanted to cry.

Finally, shivering with the cold and exhaustion, she sat down at the base of a tree. Not even sure she would survive the night, she couldn't stop the tears from falling as she stifled a sob. Had it been a mistake to leave? Would she have been safer to stay in the warm cabin in a soft bed?

Warmer, yes. Safer, no. Her life had ended when Joel had kidnapped her and brought her there by force. And then the abuse she had endured at his hands. She rubbed her cheek where he had slapped her earlier that afternoon. No, she had to get away, no matter what, even if she died trying.

Sounds of the woods filled the air. Strange sounds that spooked her. Scampering of tiny paws, buzzing of insects, rustling of leaves … she had no idea what was out there. She hoped she would make it through the night. But even if she did, then what? How would she get out?

She fingered the small gold butterfly in her pocket. Yes, she needed to believe in herself. She needed to believe that she would be okay.

After another hour, fatigue overtook her, and she lightly dozed on and off throughout the night. As the weak light of a dawning sunrise began to light up the area, she startled herself awake. She slowly stretched and then stood up, her body cold, stiff, and achy.

Looking around, she tried to get her bearings. The ground was level where she was, but it looked like it sloped downward a few yards farther away. As she carefully listened, she heard the sound of rushing water. A stream? A river? She wasn't sure. But the sound gave her something to head toward.

After Katy walked a short distance, a swiftly flowing river became visible. She realized her mouth was exceedingly dry, and at least she could get some water to drink.

Stepping carefully, she eased her way down to the river. Being more exposed there, she knew she would need to be fast and then get back to the safety of the woods. After glancing around to make sure she was alone, she carefully bent forward, cupped some water in her hands, and sipped it. It was icy cold, but it refreshed her and gave her energy. She drank more and then gently washed her face with the frigid water.

Her nerves getting to her, she quickly moved back to where the trees gave her cover and more security, and she sat down against a tree to think. Should she follow the river? And if so, in which direction? Where was the way out?

The sound of rustling in the leaves behind her startled her, and she tensed. Was that Joel? Had he found her? Her heart pounded and terror flooded her body as she pulled her knees up, trying to make herself smaller and less of a target.

A metallic jingling sound reached her. *What was that?* She gasped and then remained silent and unmoving. A dog suddenly came into view—a beautiful, silky, golden retriever stood in front of her, wagging its tail. It barked once and then sat down in front of her. As she stared at the dog, wondering where it came from, two men appeared behind the dog. "Good dog, Bailey," one of the men called out.

The other man looked at Katy. "Are you Katy?"

She nodded. "Yes." Her voice sounded hoarse.

"Good. We've been looking for you. I'm Kent, and this is Brad. We've had a search party scouring the area for the past two days." He gestured at her. "Are you okay? Are you injured?"

"I'm okay. Just cold, exhausted, and hungry." She slowly stood up, realizing she also was weak. "How did you know to look for me? Or where to find me?"

"Your friend Jennifer reported you missing, and she gave the sheriff's office enough information that they researched your boyfriend, discovered a cabin belonging to his family, and suspected you might be in this area. We are a volunteer search team working with the sheriff's office. Bailey here," he added, gesturing at the dog, "is well trained and effective at finding missing people."

Katy nodded. "But my boyfriend Joel ... he ..."

"The deputy sheriffs are up at the cabin right now looking for him."

"Joel might be out trying to find me." She glanced around at the woods. "I snuck out of the cabin last night." She shuddered as she thought about it.

Kent glanced around and then took a few steps closer. "Let's get you out of here. Can you walk okay?"

"Yes, I think so."

"Good. Follow me. Stay close."

Katy followed Kent, while Brad and Bailey brought up the rear, Brad keeping watch behind her. She began to feel safer and couldn't wait to get out of the woods. Maybe she would be safe after all.

"There you are!" Joel's booming voice cut through the air. "She's coming with me," he yelled, coming toward them as he threateningly jabbed a large pipe in the air.

Kent raised his arms in a calming gesture. "Hey, put the pipe down, we just want to talk."

"No talk. She's my girl, and she's coming back with me."

Katy whimpered, shook her head, and took a few steps back.

"Come on," Kent continued. "Just put it down."

"No!" Joel switched the pipe to his left hand and hastily raised a weapon with his right hand. He waved it back and forth toward the group.

Bailey growled.

"Down, Bailey," Brad said to the dog.

Kent stepped farther away from the group. "Hey, no need for weapons. We just want to talk."

Joel seemed determined. "Katy, come here," he demanded.

Katy shook her head. "No, Joel. I'm not going anywhere with you."

Joel stepped forward aggressively, aiming the gun at Katy.

Bailey gave one loud bark.

Joel turned his attention to the dog, his weapon beginning to move toward Bailey.

Kent, now a few steps closer to Joel, tossed a rock at Joel. Joel lurched and stepped back. His hand came up, the gun fired, and Katy shrieked.

Taking advantage of the distraction, Kent dove at Joel, tackling him to the ground. They wrestled for a couple of minutes, and then Kent pinned him to the ground. He twisted Joel's hand, causing Joel to grunt and loosen his grip on the gun. Kent grabbed Joel's gun and tossed it out of reach.

Brad got out his radio and called the deputy sheriffs. "We got them—we have both Joel and Katy. But we need some help here. Katy is safe and Joel is restrained. He was armed." He gave coordinates and then clicked off. He turned to his partner. "They're on the way." He then looked around. "Anyone hurt? Where did that bullet go?"

Terror and shock ran through Katy. Shaking, she glanced around. Then she noticed a red streak on her left arm and she gasped, her eyes widening as she stared at it. "I ... I ..."

Brad peered at her arm. "Yep, the bullet grazed your arm. It's not deep, but it should get cleaned and be looked at."

Bailey gazed up at Katy and whimpered. Brad patted the dog on his back. "It's okay, Bailey," he said calmly. "Good dog."

Katy nodded numbly as she looked at her arm and then stared at Joel pinned underneath Kent. *He had shot her!* How could she have ever dated him at all? Horror gripped her as she realized how close that was and how much worse it easily could have been.

She turned to Brad. "He would have killed me."

Brad nodded. "That is very likely. I'm really glad you're okay." He gestured at his partner. "Kent here is the best partner.

He's ex-military and knows what he's doing. I'm very grateful he's on our side and is one of the good guys. And yes, this definitely could have been a lot worse." He looked up at the sound of voices and movement. "Good. Here are the deputy sheriffs."

The taller of the two deputy sheriffs immediately went to Kent and Joel. The deputy sheriff took out handcuffs and slapped them on Joel's wrists. "Do you have any other weapons on you?" he asked Joel.

"None of your business," Joel responded.

The deputy sheriff went through Joel's pockets, carefully removing a switchblade knife. He dropped it into a plastic bag his shorter partner was holding out toward him. He then brought Joel to a standing position. "What were you trying to do here?"

Joel remained quiet.

The shorter officer and the rescue crew spoke quietly among themselves for a few minutes, and Katy glanced at them and then stared at her injured arm, unable to say a word.

The taller officer held onto Joel while the shorter one approached Katy. "We will need to get a statement from you and ask you a few questions. Can you come down to the station?"

"Yes, sure." She had many questions to ask them, but couldn't yet form the words.

"Good. Then we'll get that arm looked at and taken care of." He turned to his partner. "Let's pick up that gun over there, look for the bullet, and then we need to close off this entire area. Let's get it all roped off—this is now a crime scene." He placed a marker on a tree to identify the area, radioed dispatch, and then the two deputy sheriffs walked Joel through the woods toward their vehicle as the taller one read Joel his rights.

"Come on," Kent said to Katy. "Let's get you out of here."

Feeling shaky and woozy, Katy walked with Kent and Brad through the woods toward their vehicle, the dog prancing next to them wagging his tail. Thoughts swirled in her head, overwhelming her. What had happened? She couldn't quite grasp it. Looking at the blood on her arm, she felt dizzy and her legs got wobbly and slowly gave out. A nauseating weakness overtook her as everything turned black.

A short time later, she woke up, groggy and confused. *Where was she?* Suddenly she remembered and her eyes flew open. "Joel!"

Brad was wrapping a bandage around her arm. "Hey, you're awake. Good. Don't worry, you're safe." Brad watched her as she sat up in the back seat of their vehicle. "You feeling okay?"

Katy nodded. "Yes, just a bit weak. I'm sorry."

He handed her a bottle of water. "Nothing to apologize for. I cleaned the wound and you're all bandaged up. But I'd like to get you to a hospital to be checked and make sure everything is good."

"Okay." She sipped the water and then looked up at Brad. "And Joel?"

"He's in custody at the sheriff's office, with multiple charges pending."

Katy let out a long, slow breath. "Thank you." She let Brad secure the seatbelt around her. Bailey was buckled into the seat next to her, and he wagged his tail when she looked at him.

Brad then climbed into the front passenger seat and Kent started the vehicle and pulled out of the parking area.

As the vehicle moved forward, Katy swallowed hard. She was finally free of him. Memories of the past week flooded her, increasing her anxiety, as her arm throbbed. She pushed those thoughts aside and tried to relax.

She vowed to trust her instincts about people from now on. She was grateful Jennifer had called authorities. Her friend had warned her about Joel, but she didn't listen. She needed to listen to her friend more and trust her as well as herself. And it would be a while before she dated anyone again.

She slowly played with the small gold butterfly in her pocket. "Thank you, Aunt May," she whispered. "Yes, I will believe in myself."

She leaned her head back against the headrest, closed her eyes, and sighed. It would take a while to recover, but she was finally safe. And free.

~~~

DANCE CLASS

Stephanie Adams put down the picture of her mom and sighed. Now eight months after her mom had passed away, Stephanie still found it hard to look at her pictures. Sometimes the grief overwhelmed her. After talking with her mom a few times every week for many years, a huge empty hole was left by her mom's absence. Over the years, her mom had become her best friend, and now there were times she didn't know how she could go on without her.

Maybe if she still had a boyfriend, things would be easier and she wouldn't feel so lost. But Gary had broken up with her a month ago, and sometimes the silence and emptiness were too much to bear.

Shaking her head, Stephanie stood up and went into the kitchen. She needed to break the overwhelming despair and sadness that seemed to consume her. Maybe she should bake something. That always made her feel better, and an apple pie sounded perfect.

As she peeled and sliced the apples, memories of baking with her mom came back to her. All the pies, cakes, and cookies they baked together—it always felt like love. Now, working in the kitchen and preparing the pie crust, she no longer felt so lost.

A warmth enveloped her as she began pouring the filling into the pie crust, and she paused, thinking how much better it would be if her mom were with her.

Lifting the pie to put it in the oven, Stephanie heard her mom's voice fill her head.

Don't forget the foil around the edges to prevent the crust from burning.

Stephanie stopped short and looked around the empty kitchen, almost expecting her mom to be right there. She shook her head. Her imagination was getting away from her.

Her mom had been a teacher and always loved to teach and guide people, even at home. Now it felt like her mom was still there guiding her. But that was crazy. Her mom wasn't there. Stephanie added the foil to the crust edges, as her mom had reminded her, and then placed the pie in the oven.

As she waited for the pie to bake, grief overwhelmed her, and she broke down in sobs. Finally, her chest aching, she wiped her eyes and let out a long breath. Her mom's voice filled her head. *I am still with you.*

Stephanie looked up into the air. "Mom, are you really here? I need you. I don't want to be here without you."

I am here. Enjoy your life. Live as much as possible.

"But nothing's the same since you're not here." Stephanie stood up and paced in the kitchen. What was she doing having a conversation with someone who had passed? She shook her head and checked on the pie, removing the foil from the edges, so it could all brown nicely as it finished baking.

Stephanie sighed, went to the bathroom sink, and splashed water on her face. She needed to get control of her emotions and stay in the present. Getting lost in grief was not helping. She closed her eyes. She had to stop imagining her mom was still there talking to her.

As she dried her face with a towel, she glanced in the mirror and checked the sore on her cheek that had not been healing. It had been there at least two months and still had not healed, and it was beginning to worry her. Why wasn't it healing? What was it? What was she supposed to do?

Her mom's voice came through. *See a doctor.*

"What? Mom, is that really you? Are you here with me? Do I have cancer?"

I am here. It needs to be seen and removed.

Stephanie shuddered. She had to be imagining all of it. Was she that delusional?

The oven timer buzzed, and she smelled the enticing aroma of apple and cinnamon that now filled the house. She took the pie out of the oven, admired the golden brown crust, and placed it on the counter to cool.

Feeling out of it and not sure if she was hallucinating or not, she thought maybe she should find something to keep her busy. Sitting around and moping was not helping anything, especially without a boyfriend. And her best friend Lizzie was not available that much anymore, as she was now involved with someone new. Stephanie was on her own, and she felt like she was drowning in a sea of sorrow. She needed to do something different.

She stepped outside, took a deep breath of cool fresh air, and grabbed the mail. As she brought the mail to the kitchen table and sat down, her mom's voice spoke to her again.

Take dance lessons.

"What? That's crazy." Now she was sure she was hallucinating. That suggestion was absurd. Now in her mid-thirties, she felt too old to start taking dance classes.

Flipping through the mail, an advertisement caught her eye. Ballroom dance lessons. She drew in a quick breath and looked at the flyer. That was too coincidental. She looked at the address of the dance studio—it wasn't far—it was less than two miles away. She read the ad again. It listed five ballroom dances that they taught, and it mentioned that this month they were teaching swing. Something about that intrigued her. And maybe that would not only get her mind off everything, but it could be fun as well.

As she read through the ad one more time, she realized there was a class that started that evening. Should she go?

Go, her mom's voice said, the words reverberating in her mind.

Stephanie looked around. There was nothing else pressing that she needed to do at home. Bills and laundry could wait. Maybe it was time to have a little fun and enjoy her life a bit more. She definitely needed more of that. Maybe her mom was right.

After a light, early dinner, she thought about the dance class, and worry bubbled in her gut. Was she too old for this? As she cleaned up the kitchen, she began to feel uncertain about it all. Second thoughts ate at her, and she debated with herself if this was the right thing to do.

Go, her mom's voice said again.

Feeling her mom's urging, Stephanie decided to give it a try, and she finally got ready for the class.

A short time later, nervous and her palms damp, she hesitantly walked into the dance studio. Three other couples were practicing dance moves around the wooden floor. One young man about her own age stood awkwardly at the side, watching them.

A young, slender woman with short, dark brown hair approached her. "Hi, I'm Meg. Welcome to the dance studio. Is this your first time?"

Stephanie nodded. "Yes, I saw your flyer in the mail."

"Good, good. Welcome. I teach many styles of dance here, but this month our focus is on swing dance. Have you danced before?"

Stephanie shrugged. "Well, a little ... I ..."

Meg waved her hand, cutting her off. "It's fine. Even if you don't have experience, I can teach you. Please sign in here." She pushed a clipboard toward Stephanie. "For today, most of our students are coupled off, so you will be dancing with Josh over there. He's taken quite a few lessons already, and he can help you as we go. Are you ready to begin?"

Stephanie shrugged again and glanced around the studio dance floor. "I guess so ..."

Fifteen minutes later, she stood with Josh, in the proper dance position, smiling nervously. Meg went over the rock step, triple step, and a few other basic swing moves a few times. Josh was quiet, but he helped guide her. As they practiced to the music, Stephanie saw that he was a good dancer and a gentle teacher when she messed up.

Within a half hour, the dance steps began to feel more familiar and comfortable, and Josh led her around the dance floor, confidently leading her as they practiced the moves to the lively swing music. Every now and then Stephanie missed a step, and both of them laughed before trying again. He was easy to dance with, and Stephanie began to get more comfortable with the steps.

Thirty minutes later, Meg called Josh over to help show a new dance move. As Stephanie watched Meg and Josh perform the steps, she realized how good of a dancer Josh really was. He easily and expertly danced with the teacher, moving sensually as he danced. They danced so well together, Stephanie began to wonder how he could possibly be happy dancing with her after that. She could never dance that well, and a tinge of jealousy ran through her as she watched them.

Josh then rejoined Stephanie and smiled at her reassuringly. "You'll get this, don't worry," he said, his eyes sparkling. He took her hand, leading her into the proper position, as a tingle ran up her arm and down into her belly. As they danced and practiced the new step, she realized she didn't want the night to end. She enjoyed dancing with Josh more than she expected.

Over the remaining hour, as they danced to faster paced music, she was amazed at how comfortable she felt with him and how quickly and easily that happened. He was patient and kind, and he had a warm smile that lit up his eyes. He also was a strong leader on the dance floor, and he made it easy to follow him and get the steps right.

She was sorry when Meg turned off the music and thanked everyone for being there. Stephanie knew she wanted to take more classes. She already couldn't wait for the next class, and she hoped Josh would be there too.

As Stephanie gathered her things and got ready to leave, Josh approached her. "I really enjoyed dancing with you," he said softly.

Stephanie smiled. "I did too. That was really fun. And you're a good, strong lead. You make it easy to follow and learn the steps."

Josh's lips curved up in a shy smile. "Thank you. You picked up the dance moves very easily." He hesitated and then gestured toward her. "You remind me of someone."

"I do? Who?"

Josh smiled. "An English teacher I used to have. She was my favorite teacher. I learned so much from her. And most of all, she taught me to believe in myself."

"She sounds like an amazing teacher. What was her name?"

Josh's face filled with warmth as he thought back. "Mrs. Adams. Beatrice Adams. I'll never forget her."

Stephanie gasped and stared at Josh. "That's ... that's my mom."

Josh's eyes widened. "It is? She's your mom?"

"Yes. Well, she passed away a few months ago, but that's my mom."

His face showed compassion and concern. "I'm so sorry. She was an incredible teacher."

"Thank you, that is very kind of you to say."

He glanced behind him at the dance studio and then looked back at Stephanie. "Um, I need to get going, but, um ... would you like to have lunch with me tomorrow?"

Stephanie felt her face flush. "Yes, I'd like that."

Relief and elation flashed across Josh's face. "Great! Could I have your number?"

"Sure." She recited her number and Josh quickly entered it in his cell phone.

"Thank you." He put his cell phone in his pocket. "I know a great place for lunch. And they have good apple pie there, too."

Stephanie laughed. "That's so weird that you mention that. I just baked an apple pie this afternoon. In fact, it's my mom's recipe. She taught me a lot. Always the teacher," she added, laughing again.

Josh's face lit up. "I love apple pie—it's my favorite."

They walked out of the dance studio together and paused on the walkway in the cool evening air. Josh turned to her. "You do resemble your mom and you have similar mannerisms. You seem like a caring and kind person, too. Just like her."

Stephanie smiled. "Thank you." Feeling awkward, she felt her face flush.

"Is twelve noon good for you tomorrow? Can I pick you up?"

"Yes, that would be great. I live just a couple miles from here." She pointed in the general direction and, as she moved her arm, her purse fell to the ground.

Josh immediately squatted to pick it up for her, and Stephanie quickly leaned forward reaching for it. As Josh rose with the purse in his hand, their heads bumped together.

"Oh!" Stephanie cried out.

"Oh, I'm so sorry," Josh replied, reaching for Stephanie to hold her steady. "Are you okay?"

Stephanie felt slightly off balance and stepped forward, bumping into Josh. "Oh, I'm sorry, I'm such a klutz today."

Josh laughed as he held her stable and handed her the purse. "You're fine." He laughed again. "I think you're just trying to find a way to have another dance with me."

Stephanie laughed and shook her head. "I have to remember it's triple step, not triple trip and fall."

Josh laughed. "That is too funny." His eyes sparkled as he laughed. "And you're a good dancer—really. You learned the steps very quickly." He glanced at his watch. "I'm sorry, but I really need to get going. I'll call you tomorrow before I pick you up, okay?"

"Yes, thank you. I look forward to it."

He smiled, his face radiating warmth. "Me too." He squeezed her hand, sending a shiver up her arm, and then he turned and headed to his car.

Stephanie watched him walk, a warm feeling filling her gut. The evening had become much more than she could have anticipated, and she felt her spirits lift.

She got in her car and started the engine. "Thanks, Mom," she said to the air around her. "Dance lessons was a really good idea. How did you know? Do you remember Josh? Did you know he'd be there? He spoke so highly of you."

I remember Josh. He is a very kind and special man. He is good for you.

"Mom, you made an impact on so many people, including me. Thanks for guiding me and for still helping me. I love you, Mom."

I will always be here with you. And don't forget to see a doctor for that sore on your cheek.

Stephanie laughed. "Yes, Mom." She chuckled as she drove home.

She looked forward to the next day. Maybe after lunch she would invite Josh inside her home for some homemade apple pie. And maybe they could practice the dance steps too.

She felt a smile grow on her face. It seemed that life really could turn around. Her mom was still with her, and things were definitely looking up.

~~~

Turning Point

A ndrea trembled with fear. She knew John would be angry
again. Lately he seemed to always be angry. Things needed
to be perfect for him to be happy, and this was an imperfect
world. And people weren't perfect, either. But he somehow
couldn't understand that.

And now dinner was going to be late, and the potatoes
would not be ready at the same time as the chicken. She knew he
would scream and yell at her, and she was so tired of his anger.

Here it comes, she thought, as he entered the kitchen.

John glared at her, his face red and contorted with rage. "You
bitch!" he bellowed, his eyes cutting into her. "You know I want
dinner on time!"

Andrea simply watched him, saying nothing. *Let him yell, and
it will be over soon,* she thought.

He took a menacing step toward her, his eyes fuming. Her
skin prickled as she took in the fury radiating from the man in
front of her. In a quick motion, his hand drew back and then came
forward, slapping her across the face so hard her head snapped
back. Then he punched her in the stomach, knocking the wind out
of her. In shock, unable to breathe, with pain radiating throughout
her body, she collapsed to the floor.

Struggling to breathe and make sense out of what just
happened, she barely heard his furious rant as he continued to

yell at her. She clutched her belly and took small breaths as tears stung her eyes. Another jolt of intense pain hit her as his hard shoe rammed into her side. Shock and pain overwhelmed her. She stayed crumpled in a tight ball, waiting for another impact. But instead of another blow, his angry voice assaulted her. "When I come back, dinner better be on the table!" He stormed out, slamming the door behind him.

She remained in a fetal position for a long time. When she could finally breathe normally again, sobs took over. What happened? He had never hit her before.

And he never would again. This was it. She was through.

She stood up, one hand on her aching belly, and scribbled a quick note asking him to leave and be gone by morning. Then she grabbed a few belongings and rushed down to the apartment building's parking garage to her car.

As she reached it, terror flooded her as John suddenly appeared. He walked over to her and glared at her.

"Where are you going?" he demanded, venom in his voice. "I want dinner."

"I'm going out. And I'm through with you. I want you gone before morning. I never want to see you again." Her voice shook, but she meant every word.

"What?" he bellowed, taking a menacing step toward her. "You deserved it. It was all your fault. You bitch!" Enraged, he took another step toward her and reached out to grab her.

Terrified, she jumped back, out of his reach, as he stood there glaring at her. Her hand trembling, she opened her car door and then faced him.

"No." Her voice was stronger now. "I'm done. I want you gone." She quickly got in her car before he could stop her, pulled the door shut, and locked it as he lunged forward and grabbed for the handle.

Shaking, she backed up as he screamed at her, and then she eased the car up the ramp from the parking garage and drove off, not even glancing back.

Pulling in at a nearby motel, she checked in, went to her assigned room, and collapsed on the bed. What happened? What had gotten into him? When had things changed? She could not understand any of it. Numb at first, she finally broke down and sobbed for hours.

The tears slowly subsided, and Andrea let out a long sigh. Maybe this was a good thing. It finally propelled her to leave him. She should have left him long ago. She was sick of his constant criticism and complaints. Nothing she did was ever good enough. And after hearing his put-downs day after day, she had started believing his words. She felt unimportant and worthless. This was not the life she wanted.

Did other couples fight and yell all the time? Did they cry every day too? Was this what life was like for all couples? Was romantic love and real happiness just in the movies? She wasn't sure. She just knew she couldn't live like that anymore. She couldn't even remember the last time she really felt happy. Or laughed.

There was a time she liked who she was. She needed to get that back. He had destroyed her self-esteem and her happiness. There was never any peace anymore. She never wanted to see him again. She hoped he would be gone when she returned home the next day.

After a night of not sleeping, she rubbed her swollen and burning eyes. Looking in the mirror, she saw her red, puffy eyes and the bruises on her face and her side. If he wasn't gone, she would go straight to the police and file charges.

Trembling, she drove home slowly, not knowing what to expect. Would he be gone? Or would he be even angrier? Would he try to kill her? As she pulled into the parking garage, she noticed his car was gone. Did he leave for a while to get something? Or was he gone for good?

She slowly went up to their apartment. Her hand shook as she put the key in the lock and opened the door. Silence greeted her.

A note was left on the counter, and she picked it up with trembling fingers. Tears filled her eyes as she read it.

> *I'm leaving you. But not because you asked me to. I'm leaving because I deserve someone much better than you. You are worthless, and you don't deserve someone as good as me. I should never have wasted my time with you. I'm taking the first flight out and I never want to see you again. John*

Her eyes burned with tears, and she swallowed hard past the lump in her throat. He always had to have the last dig. But she didn't care. She just wanted him gone.

Had he really left? She quickly ran into their bedroom. His clothes were gone. His dresser drawers were empty. She bit her lower lip as a small smile started forming and tears trailed down her cheeks.

The apartment was quiet. It felt strange. No yelling, no criticism, no complaints. She ran downstairs and went outside in flip-flops and no one yelled at her for that.

She looked up at the clear blue sky and saw a plane pass overhead. Was he on that flight? It didn't matter. As long as he was gone.

She went back in and looked around the apartment. Her dirty coffee mug sat on the counter and no one screamed at her about it. A rush of fear ran through her, but then she decided to leave it there for another hour, and a strangled giggle came out.

Quickly glancing around to make sure no one was there to yell at her, she let out a long breath. Her body began to relax in the empty silence. She felt warmth settle around her. Was this what peace was like?

She knew she still needed to heal and recover from this, but she felt good that she had taken the first step toward a better life, and she was determined to learn to love herself again. And maybe one day someone else would love her too, exactly as she was.

But for now, she was finally at peace. She felt her lips curl up in a small, shaky, timid smile, and it began settling in that life was becoming good again. She washed her coffee mug and defiantly placed it crooked on the drying tray, smiling wider, as a deep sense of peace permeated the room.

Then she settled in on the recliner and started humming, something she had not done in years, and she knew she would be okay.

~~~

BECOMING WHOLE

A restless unease moved through Emma as she joined her family for dinner. Tomorrow she would turn eighteen, and her birthday always brought a sense of agitation. She knew it should be a happy day, but it was usually filled with increased apprehension.

She always knew she was adopted, and an underlying feeling of loss and rejection filtered through her life, even though her parents were loving and kind. Her family was nice to her, but she had lingering anxiety and a nagging feeling that she simply did not fit in. Her light brown hair and blue eyes did not look like either of her parents or her sister. But more than that, she always wondered why she had been given away, and she longed for a place where she really felt she belonged, and that longing filled her with guilt.

Nervous and dreading her birthday the next day, her stomach ached as she sat at the kitchen table for dinner and stared at her food.

"Are you okay, Emma?" Her mom looked at her. "Are you feeling sick?"

Emma shook her head. "I'm just uncomfortable about tomorrow. I guess I just don't like birthdays or all the fuss."

Her mother nodded. "I know, sweetheart. We won't do anything big, but I have your favorite cake for you—red velvet cake with cream cheese frosting."

"Thank you. I love that cake." She gave a weak smile and pushed her food around on the plate, and then picked at her food and slowly ate.

Dinner finally finished, she pushed away from the table and ran to her room. She hated her birthday. It was another reminder that her birth mom had given her away, that she was not wanted, and her anxiety grew. Trying to calm down and slow her breathing, she looked around the bedroom. There was not much. A few books, her guitar, and a notebook where she wrote poetry. A few treasured stuffed animals from her childhood sat on her dresser. An emptiness gnawed at her, and she blinked back the tears.

After a restless night of dozing on and off, she crept into the kitchen the next morning for breakfast.

Her mother was making pancakes and she turned and smiled at Emma. "Happy birthday, honey. Want some pancakes? I know that's your favorite for breakfast, so I wanted to make that for you."

Emma sniffed the air, loving the smell that filled the kitchen. "Thank you. I do like your pancakes."

"I know, sweetie. Here, the pancakes are ready." She placed the plate on the table and Emma inhaled the homey aroma before digging in. Maybe the day wouldn't be so bad.

As Emma began to push away from the table after finishing her breakfast, her mom sat down across from her. "I have something special to give you. When we adopted you, your birth mother gave the adoption agency a small box of items for you for when you turned eighteen. We promised that we would hold it for you until then. And now that you are eighteen, you can have it. I don't know what's in it, but it's for you from your birth mother."

Emma's mouth fell open and she stared at her mom.

"Wait here and I'll go get it." Her mom left the room, and Emma stared after her. Her stomach churned. What could be in the box? Would she find the answers to her questions? She tapped her foot as fear flooded her system.

A couple of minutes later, her mom returned carrying a small box, and she placed it on the table. "Here, honey. This is the box. Take your time." She pushed the light blue cardboard box toward Emma. "And please know that no matter what is in it and what you want to do, we support you and always love you, and you are always part of our family. And if you want to talk about it, I'm here for you. Okay?"

Emma nodded and whispered, "Thank you." She grabbed the cardboard box and ran up to her room.

Nervous and jittery, Emma sat on the bed and stared at the box. She wiped her damp hands on her jeans and, hands shaking, she slowly untied the old, wrinkled ribbon and lifted the lid. After a moment's hesitation, her fingers trembling, she peeked in the box and carefully removed the contents. There were a few letters, some pictures, and a small, pink ribbon.

Her heart pounding, she picked up the pictures and gasped, peering intently at the photos. A teenaged girl, holding a baby wrapped in a pink blanket, smiled at the camera. There were a few pictures of the baby, some with a pink ribbon in her hair—the same pink ribbon that was in the box. Emma's heart thudded in her chest as she studied the pictures again.

On the back of the baby pictures were written her name and a date. She felt her throat close up. These were pictures of her as a baby—she was a few weeks old in two pictures, and one month old in one of the pictures. The young woman, who must be her birth mom, looked just like her. Emma felt a deep soul yearning building inside. She was actually looking at a photo of her biological mother and herself as a baby. Why did her birth mom give her away? Did she still remember her? Did she ever think about her?

Her hands shook as she put the photos down and opened the letter. She began to read, struggling to breathe, as tears fell.

My sweet baby Emma,

I love you so much and I wish I could give you the life you deserve. But I cannot, and you deserve the best life possible.

I am only seventeen and am not able to care for you. I wish things were different, but they are not in my control. I love you so deeply but I am not able to keep you or take care of you. After a month of agonizing over it, I have reached the difficult decision that I need to give you up for adoption. I desperately hope you will have a loving home and will have a better life than anything I can offer. I hope and trust this is the right thing to do.

Emma looked away and then fell forward, sobs wracking her body. She had to keep reading, but it was hard to focus. Her mouth dry, she wiped her tears away and continued reading.

My parents drink too much and we have no money. Your dad was my boyfriend in high school, but we are no longer together. This is such a difficult decision, and I wish I could keep you. It hurts me so bad to give you away, but I really have no choice. Please know that I love you with every fiber of my being and I will always love you.

I hope you will be happy, and I hope one day you can forgive me.

With Love, your mother, Claire

By the time Emma finished reading the letter, she was sobbing and gasping for air.

For a few minutes, Emma could barely breathe. Then she looked through the other letters. In one of the letters, Claire said she played the guitar and wrote poetry—just like her! There was more information about her birth family and contact information if Emma wished to reach out to her. If the information was still valid, Emma would be able to reach her.

Fear gripped her. Would Claire still want to be contacted eighteen years after she wrote the letter? Would she still remember her? Or was she long forgotten? Would her birth mom want to meet her now? Or was she a bad memory of a difficult time? Was she even still alive?

Emma held the letter to her chest. The yearning inside grew too strong, and she knew she desperately needed to call and try to meet her birth mom. Claire would probably be about 35 now. Her heart ached as a rush of fear, anxiety, desperation, and conflicting feelings rushed through her. Should she call?

Clutching the letters and photos, Emma rocked back and forth, sobbing, trying to muster the courage to make the phone call.

After an hour, she could no longer hold back. Hands shaking, she called the number scrawled on one of the letters, hoping Claire was still at the same number.

The call was answered on the second ring. "Hello?"

Emma could barely speak, and her voice was hoarse. "Um, Claire?"

"Yes?"

"Um ... I'm not sure how to ... This is Emma. I'm your daughter."

***

One week later, checking her image in the mirror, Emma ran her fingers through her light brown hair and smoothed down the yellow blouse she wore. Wearing her favorite color, she hoped it looked bright and cheery, but her nerves were getting the better of her. Her hands were sweating, and she felt jittery. Why was she so nervous? But she had to see her. She had to meet the woman who gave birth to her.

Claire's voice had been soft and hesitant on the phone when they had briefly talked, but she had agreed to meet. However, Emma sensed some reluctance. Was she reluctant because she did not really want to meet? Was this a mistake? Or was Claire simply as scared as she was? Whichever it was, Emma could not back out. This was too important, and she felt driven.

Whatever happened, she would deal with it. Even if it ended in disappointment, it was better to know than always wonder. She checked her watch again. It was time to leave.

Twenty minutes later, she pulled into the parking lot at the coffee shop and parked. She sat there unmoving for a few minutes, trying to slow down the racing of her heart. Finally, hands cold and shaking, she got out of the car and walked to the entrance of the coffee shop.

Her legs feeling rubbery, she hesitated. What if Claire didn't even show up? What if she really didn't want to see her? Maybe this was all a mistake.

Tires pulling into a parking spot got her attention, and she turned and watched a small white car pull in a few spots away from hers. A woman got out, shut and locked the car door, checked her watch, and looked around. She seemed nervous.

For some reason, this woman held Emma's attention. The woman was short, slightly built, and had light brown hair about her color. As the woman came closer, something seemed vaguely familiar. The woman approached the front entrance, stopped, and looked at Emma.

Emma saw her own blue eyes, worried, scared, and anxious, reflected in this woman's face. The woman wore a beautiful yellow blouse, a color that matched her own, and ...

Emma gasped and then held her breath.

The woman turned to her and her eyes opened wide. "Emma?"

Emma nodded, at first unable to speak. Then she finally whispered, "Claire?"

The woman nodded and opened her arms. Emma moved forward, and the two embraced, tightly holding on to each other.

When they finally pulled apart, they both had tears running down their faces. Emma looked at Claire, who was so much like herself. "Thank you for meeting me. It is so good to see you. Let's go in and have lunch and talk."

Claire dabbed at her eyes with a small tissue. "Yes, yes, let's go in."

Emma opened the door and held it for Claire, then followed her in. After being seated in a booth, looking over the menu, and ordering their meals, they relaxed and gazed at each other.

"Thank you for the box you sent when I was adopted." Emma's voice was soft. "It was nice to read the letter and see the pictures. But I was afraid to call you."

Claire's face softened. "I'm glad you got the box and I'm glad you called. I didn't know if you would be angry or resent me." She toyed with her napkin. "Emma, I loved you more than you could know. It was so hard to give you away, but I could not offer you a decent life. I could not take care of you."

"I know. I understand. Thank you for doing what you felt was best for me. And thank you for that letter. That helped a lot."

Claire reached out and squeezed Emma's hand. "I hope you had a good life and are with a good family."

"Yes, I am. My parents have been very good to me. They are loving and kind. But something has been missing in my life, and I always somehow felt lost. I always longed to find a blood relative. A place where I felt complete and where I truly belonged."

Claire nodded. "Yes, I can understand that. You're not mad at me?"

"Oh, no, no, of course not. I just always wondered why you gave me away. And reading that letter and meeting you helps a lot."

The waitress placed steaming plates of food on the table, refilled their iced tea, and then went to another table.

Claire smiled. "Do you know that I celebrate your birthday every year?"

Emma gasped. "You do?"

"Oh, yes. Each year on your birthday I get a small cake and put a candle in it and sing happy birthday to you. And every day I think of you and wonder how you're doing. I always wish I could hold you. I never stopped loving you."

Emma took a bite of her chicken sandwich and looked at her mom. "I look like you."

Claire smiled. "Yes, you do. And you are so beautiful."

Emma laughed. "Thank you. You are too." She grabbed a French fry. "And we're a lot alike, too. We both play the guitar and write poetry."

"You do that too?" She sipped her iced tea. "And look—we wore the same color."

"I know—I love yellow. It's my favorite color."

"Mine too!"

Conversation flowed easily as they shared more about themselves, opened up to each other, and gradually felt more comfortable.

As they finished their meal and pushed their plates forward, Emma saw worry in her mother's face. "What's wrong? I can see you're worried about something."

"It's nothing. I—"

"Tell me. Please."

Claire blinked and looked away for a few moments, then looked back at Emma. "You're the only remaining family I have. My parents are gone, and there's no one else. I don't want to lose you again."

Emma grabbed Claire's hands. "I'm not going anywhere. You're also the only blood relative I have. I want you in my life. We need each other."

***

A week later, Emma went downstairs to the kitchen for breakfast. Her adoptive mom was making omelets and turned to her. "Hi, honey. How is it going with your birth mom? Is that going well? Did you want to talk about it? Would you like an omelet?"

"It's good. We have a lot in common and it feels good deep down to connect with her. It means a lot." She sat at the kitchen table. "But you're still important too. You're my family," she quickly added. "And yes, I'd love an omelet, thank you."

"I want you to know that I'm proud of you for having the courage to reach out to your birth mother, and I'm glad that's going well. And please know that I love and support you. Please don't forget that you're an important part of this family too." She blinked. "You're my baby, too."

Emma felt heat rising in her face. "Thank you. I know. And I do feel a little guilty, like I'm betraying you." She shook her head. "You're not upset that I contacted her?"

Her mom set a plate with the omelet on the table and then sat down across from Emma. "Not at all. This is a big thing, and I know it's important to you. And if it's important to you, then it's important to me. I don't want to lose you, but I also don't want to hold you back from what you need to do. You do what you feel is right. Just know that we love you, you are part of our family, and you are always welcome here. I want what's best for you."

"Thank you." Emma sighed. "Claire has no other family—just me. And I'd like to develop more of a relationship with her."

"Hey, why don't I invite her here? I would love to meet her, if that's okay with you. And she's welcome here as well."

Emma looked up at her. "Really? Thank you, Mom. That is really nice. I really appreciate you being okay with all this."

"I love you, sweetheart. I want you to be happy. I know this is important to you."

Emma blinked tears away as her eyes burned, and she could not speak for a few moments. Finally she looked up. "Thank you.

You will always be my mom, and I love you. Thank you for supporting all this."

"You're welcome. Claire can be part of our family, too."

Emma wiped away a tear. "It feels like instead of not quite belonging, I now belong to two families. Or maybe our family just got bigger." She smiled. "And I feel complete now. I finally feel like I am whole and I really belong. Thank you, Mom."

"You're welcome, sweetheart. How's the omelet?"

Emma laughed, an overwhelming sense of relief, gratitude, and wholeness flooding her. "The omelet is great. Thank you." She laughed again. "I think I'm going to be okay now."

~~~

PINK JELLY BEANS

Soft silence settled in the woods, and I shivered in the cold, bunching the coat tighter around me. I glanced around, then followed her footsteps which showed erratically in the blanket of snow. I whispered a quick prayer that she was okay.

Her footsteps suddenly seemed to turn in different directions, went in a small circle, and then went straight again. I knew she was confused. She would not survive long out here. Besides easily getting lost in these woods, she could freeze to death, and I had to find her as quickly as possible. *Please be safe. Please.*

Even if she had a coat on, I knew she must be shivering and cold, and she might not even have a coat. I was grateful there was snow on the ground so that at least there were footprints to follow and I could find her more easily. This was the second time she had wandered off from the memory-care facility. I would have to talk to them again about locking the doors or putting an alarm wristband on her so they would be alerted if she tried to leave the facility.

Then I saw her—she was leaning against a tree, humming, and picking up the hem of her pink flowered nightgown.

"Mom!" I called. She turned toward me, a bewildered look on her face. "Mom, let me get you back home."

She squinted at me. "Who are you?"

My voice caught in my throat. "I'm your daughter," I whispered, tears burning my eyes. "I need to get you back home."

My mom giggled. "My name's Margaret. I'm just going to the store for some jelly beans, silly."

"Mom, no, please." I shivered as the frigid air pressed into me. How was my mother not cold? "Mom, I'll give you jelly beans when we get back home. All the jelly beans you want, I promise."

"The pink ones?"

"Yes, yes, the pink ones, any kind you want." All I wanted was to get her back inside, safe and warm.

She squinted at me. "I don't know who you are, but the bus will be here any minute."

I choked on my words. "Mom, no. There's no bus ... I mean, the bus is late. I'll take you where you need to go."

My mother stared at me and then flounced her nightgown. "Do you like my nightgown?"

"Yes, it's pretty, I—"

"Who did you say you were?"

"Mom, I'm your daughter. I want to help you."

"My name is Margaret. I have a daughter but she's still a baby. She's five."

My voice was barely audible. "That's me, Mom. I've grown up."

She smiled with pride. "Her name is Ellie."

"Yes, Mom. My name is Ellie."

"It is?" She chuckled. "That's a funny coincidence."

"Mom, let me take you to the bus stop. I'll get you some jelly beans, and you can see Ellie."

My mom's face lit up. "I would love that. Thank you, dear, whoever you are. You're very nice."

I nodded and reached for her. "Come with me. I'll help you."

She stepped toward me, the snow crunching under her fuzzy pink slippers. "Okay," she said in a sing-song voice as she reached her hand toward me.

I reached out and took her hand in mine. "This way, Mom. The bus and the jelly beans and Ellie are all this way, waiting for you."

"Oh, good." She walked by my side as I led her back down the snowy path toward the memory-care facility. "Do you know I just got back from Las Vegas?"

"Mom, you've been living in a ..." I caught myself. "You did? Was it fun?"

She laughed. "Oh, yes. We snuck out of school. Me and Richard went to Las Vegas. It was so much fun. But now we're back." She looked at me. "But you can't tell anyone. It's a secret." She giggled and raised a finger to her lips indicating I should keep her secret.

"Yes, of course. I won't tell anyone."

"Oh, good. You're very nice. You would like Ellie. You're a lot like her. Did you know she wants to be a nurse when she grows up? She'll graduate high school next year."

I squeezed my mom's cold hand as we continued down the snowy path. My heart thudded in my chest and I ached for her. "That's nice. That's a good field to go into. I'm sure she'll do very well."

She looked at me and gave a small, shy smile. "Can you take me to the grocery store? I don't remember where I parked my car, and I need to go get groceries."

"Yes, Mom, I'll take you there next week."

"Oh, good. You're very nice. You'd like Ellie. I'm sure you would be great friends. But she's still a little girl."

I sucked in a deep breath. "I'm sure she loves you very much." Weren't her feet ice cold? I hoped she wouldn't get frostbite.

"Well, I sure love her. Even though she gets into my makeup and doesn't think I know about it." She snickered.

I gasped. She knew about that? I never knew she knew. "I know you are a very good mom to her and she loves you. She is in a wonderful family."

"Thank you, dear, that is very kind of you." She suddenly looked around. "Where are we? Why are we out in the snow? It's cold out here. What is this place?" She shivered.

I looked around at the snow gently falling. "We just went for a walk, that's all. We're almost home."

"Well, good, because it's freezing out here, and I'm late for my mahjong game." She laughed. "I always win. But now they'll wonder why I'm late."

"They'll understand. It's okay."

"Is it lunchtime yet? I'm hungry."

"It's 4:00, Mom. They'll be serving dinner in an hour."

"Oh, good. That's nice. I like the hotel we're staying in. Maybe we can go ice skating later."

"Yes, Mom. Maybe later." I led her off the main path and down a small side path, then up a few steps that led to a patio. "Here we are. This is where you live."

"It is? Where's my husband?"

I opened the door and we walked into the warm lobby. "Mom, he passed …" I hesitated and then changed what I wanted to say. There was no need to hurt her, and she wouldn't remember five minutes later anyway. "He went out for a little while. He'll be back. Let's get you settled in."

"Okay, thank you, dear. Do you work here?"

"No, I'm Ellie, your daughter, I'm here to visit you."

Her eyes lit up. "Ellie! I know you. You're my daughter! Thank you for coming to see me, I've missed you."

"I've missed you too. I love you, Mom." Tears ran down my face as a real connection was made, no matter how long it lasted. I hugged her and kissed her cheek, then stamped the snow off my shoes and walked her through the lobby.

She looked around, a bewildered look on her face. "Where are we? Is it time for breakfast? Who are you?"

"You're home, Mom. They'll serve dinner soon. Let me take you to your room and I'll let them know you're back."

I started walking her down the hallway toward her room when I heard a woman's voice call out in our direction. "Margaret! There you are!" An aide came bustling over. I checked her nametag and saw the name Pat on it. "We were looking all over for you." She looked at me. "Where was she?"

I let out my breath and tried to tamp down my anger and keep my voice steady. "She was wandering out in the snow down in the woods. This is the second time she has wandered off. The doors really need to be locked, and she needs an alarm band on her wrist so it triggers it and alerts you if she tries to leave. You need to keep her safe so she doesn't—"

Pat nodded. "Yes, yes, we know. We have the wristband for her at the front desk. She never tried to leave before on her own, so we didn't think it was needed. That other time was months ago when we had taken a small group out for a walk and she wandered off, but we don't do that anymore, we keep all the residents inside now. And she has not left the facility in a long time. But we will put the wristband on her today. I promise you, we will keep your mom safe." She watched my face and her voice softened. "Thank you for finding her and bringing her back. We looked everywhere for her. This won't happen again, I promise."

I tapped my foot. "I hope not." Then I relaxed. "Thank you. I know you take good care of her. She is just so confused and I worry about her."

Pat's voice was calm and soft. "I know. We will be making changes and taking additional steps to prevent another incident. They are already installing an audible alarm on the front door, so it will set off an alarm anytime it opens, and all the other doors will be locked and can only be opened with a special code." Her voice got quieter. "My own mother went through this, so I really do understand. Your mom will be safe here, I promise."

My mom twirled around, her pink nightgown fluttering around her legs. "Hey, when is breakfast? I'm hungry." She looked at me. "Who are you?"

Pat turned to her and spoke in a caring and loving manner. "Sweet Margaret, we'll be serving dinner in just a few minutes. We'll put warm socks on you first and then we'll go down to the dining room, okay? Come, I'll take you. You're gonna love it. They have meatloaf today, your favorite." She turned to me and smiled.

My mom looked at her. "With mashed potatoes?"

"Yes, Margaret. With mashed potatoes and gravy, just like you like them."

"Oh, good," my mom said, smiling. "I'm hungry. What are we waiting for?" Then she turned to me. "Who is that? Does she live here too? She reminds me of my daughter."

I watched Pat walk my mom down the hall toward her room.

"Bye, Mom," I whispered. "I'll bring the pink jelly beans next time I come. I love you."

~~~

GRIEF AND LOVE

Her hand trembling, for a close-up shot, Kara wiped a tear off her cheek and took a deep breath. It had now been a year since her brother had killed himself. He had been only twenty-six, two years older than she was. It still felt like it happened yesterday, and she wasn't sure she would ever get over it.

She slowly walked down the pier that stretched out over the ocean. This was where it had happened. Her brother Russ, after suffering for years with depression, finally ended his life at this spot.

Her heart heavy with grief, she stared into the water at the end of the pier. The deep blue of the water looked endless.

She should have known. She should have stopped him. Shaking her head, she felt overcome with guilt. They had been so close. Why didn't he talk to her one more time? How could she not have known?

She wished he were still here. But she couldn't go back in time, and even if she could, it would not have changed anything. Russ had made up his mind and he had not told anyone.

"Russ ..." she whispered to the water, watching the soft waves bobbing on the surface.

She gasped as the dream from last night came back to her. Russ had come to her with a message. In the dream, she had been sitting here at the end of the pier, and Russ had risen out of the water and sat next to her. "Don't blame yourself," he had told her. "It was my decision—I chose to do it. It was not your fault, and you could not have stopped me." He hugged her, the cool water seeping into her clothes. "Talk to someone. Talk to Jeremy. Live your life, Kara. Be happy. I love you." Then he faded into nothingness, and she was alone again.

The dream had seemed so real at the time. Goosebumps rose on her arms. Was that really him? Had he actually come to her in a dream? She wasn't sure, but it would be nice if he really had visited her while she slept.

Staring off over the ocean, she thought about the memories she had of her brother ... all their favorite times together. Happy and loving times.

She turned and looked behind her as footsteps approached on the pier. "Hey, Jeremy," she said, her voice cracking. Jeremy had been Russ's closest friend, and she knew he was hurting too.

"Hey, Kara." Jeremy sat next to her on the pier. "I thought you might be out here."

"It's been a year," she whispered.

"Yes. One year ago today." He shook his head. "I miss him so much. He was like a brother to me."

"I know. You two were so close and so much alike." She sighed. Jeremy was always kind to her, and she liked him more and more over the years. He was a good friend to both of them, and she was glad he was here now.

They sat in silence for a few minutes, the gentle sounds of the water soothing.

Jeremy turned to her, his voice soft. "Russ spoke of you often. He really cared about you."

Her eyes burned, and another tear ran down her cheek. "I loved him so much. I ... I can't believe he's gone."

"I know."

"I should have known. I should have been able to stop him."

Jeremy shook his head. "You couldn't have known." He stared out over the water. "And I thought the same thing. I should have known—he was my best friend. But neither of us could have known or stopped him."

"He didn't talk to you about doing something like that?"

"No, never. He mentioned feeling down or depressed every now and then, but nothing that heavy. Most of the time he seemed happy. We joked about stuff all the time." He waved his hand in the air and his voice grew quiet. "I never knew."

She sighed. "Sometimes it hurts too much. It feels like it's too much to handle."

Jeremy reached over and placed a warm hand on her back. "I understand. But he would want you to be happy."

"I know. I just—"

"You wouldn't do anything like that, would you?" His face reflected his concern.

Kara pursed her lips and looked away as more tears fell. "No, I wouldn't." She glanced at Jeremy and saw his eyes were wet. "Don't worry. This is just a tough day."

"I know. It is for me, too." He gently rubbed her back. "You know, I had a dream about Russ last night."

Kara's eyes opened wide and she stared at him. "What? You did? So did I."

Jeremy's lips trembled. "He came to me in a dream and told me it wasn't my fault, that I couldn't have known or stopped him, and to enjoy my life. He told me to be happy."

She held his gaze. "That's what he told me, too."

"And he said I should talk to you." He paused for a few moments. "That's one of the reasons I came out here today. I was hoping you would be here."

She stared at him and didn't answer right away. "He told me the same thing and that I should talk to you."

His brow furrowed. "Are you serious?"

"Yeah. I think we were the two people he was closest to."

"Maybe he thought we could support each other through this and find comfort."

"Maybe." She sighed. "But I don't know if I could find comfort anywhere right now."

Jeremy placed his arm around her shoulder and squeezed. She let out a long breath and laid her head on his shoulder. He held her against him for a long time.

Finally, Kara looked up at him. "Thank you. I think this is exactly what I needed."

"Me too." He leaned over and placed a gentle kiss on the top of her head.

Grief and longing suddenly overwhelmed her, and she turned to Jeremy. She buried her face in his chest and sobbed, letting out the feelings she had held in for too long. He wrapped his arms around her and held her tightly.

After a few minutes, Kara looked up at him and saw he had been crying too. "Thank you for being here," she whispered.

He pressed his lips together and nodded, not saying a word.

Kara glanced at him and knew he was feeling the same things she was. "Well, he wants us to be happy, but it's hard. It will take a while."

"Yes, it takes time. We'll get there."

She looked into his eyes and saw compassion and caring mixed with grief and pain. "You were a good friend to him. And now you're a good friend to me, too."

"I always cared about you." He smiled and ran his fingers along her cheek. "Would you like to get something to eat?"

She felt herself grow warm as she gazed into his soft brown eyes, sensing deep compassion and tenderness emanating from him. "Yes, I'd really like that." Feeling a close bond with him, feelings of affection and a touch of desire flowed through her, easing the feelings of grief. Maybe there was a way through this where she could heal and move forward.

Jeremy stood up, reached a hand down, and helped her get up.

Kara threw her arms around him and hugged him. "Thank you," she murmured. "You are helping me find a way to be happy again."

"You deserve to be happy. We both do." He leaned forward, hesitated, and then gently pressed his lips to hers.

She responded, kissing him back, as heat rose in her face. She watched his cheeks turn pink as he smiled back.

As they turned to walk back down the pier, Jeremy reached for her hand, and the warmth of his hand enveloping hers sent a tingle through her. She felt herself flush as she realized it felt so comfortable and natural to hold hands with him. It felt like they had been friends forever—as though they understood each other on deeper levels and always had. And in some ways, maybe that was true, as they had been around each other all those years when he was close friends with Russ.

Maybe her brother was actually helping both of them find more than just support and comfort. Maybe he saw more for them. Maybe he saw something special in their hearts. And maybe now she did too.

As they walked, Jeremy squeezed her hand, and she felt the heat go through her arm. Something new and warm began to fill her, and she felt her heart begin to soften.

Maybe she could be happy again. And maybe she could even find love—it might be very close.

~~~

FINDING SHELTER

A **backpack filled** with schoolbooks on his back, Dalton pedaled his bicycle down the residential street toward his friend's house. Only eight years old, Dalton felt uncomfortable too much of the time, even at home. Especially at home. He was grateful for Jason, his one friend in a world that seemed cold and cruel, where he always felt like an outsider.

His stomach knotted up with nerves, and he fought against tears that threatened to fill his eyes. Why did he have to be so sensitive? He wondered if his life would be different if his mother were still alive. Maybe he would at least have lunch made for him when he went to school. He hated being hungry and going to school without any lunch. His dad never made him lunch, and his belly ached just thinking about all the times he went hungry while watching other kids eat.

But the worst part was being hit so often. The screaming, the punching, the beatings ... Why did his dad hate him so much? What did he ever do wrong? He tried so hard to be good and do what he was told. But somehow he never could please his dad. Nothing he ever did was acceptable. And he had no idea why. What was wrong with him that made him so unlovable that even his own dad didn't love him?

Even when the bruises weren't visible to others, they were a constant reminder that he just wasn't good enough and never would be, and that made him hate himself and his life.

He shook his head. He couldn't think about that now. He just wanted to get to Jason's house. Jason's mom was always nice to him. Were all moms that nice? Sadness filled him as he wished he could have a nice mom at home too.

After pedaling up the driveway, he locked his bike on their porch and rang the bell. Sniffing, he wiped away one tear and tried to force a smile on his face.

The door opened and Jason stood there, his brown hair almost reaching his eyes. "Hey, Dalton. C'mon in."

Dalton followed Jason into the warm house. It felt homey and comfortable, and they entered the brightly lit kitchen.

Jason's mom turned toward him from the sink, a smile on her face, her long brown hair falling softly below her shoulders. "Hi, Dalton, how are you today? You doing okay?"

Dalton shrugged and stared at his shoes. "Yes, fine, thank you, Mrs. Daniels."

"Kate. Please call me Kate." She watched him for a moment and then continued. "We had extra food today again, so I made you a sandwich. I hope that's okay. Do you like turkey? It's a turkey sandwich with mayo, lettuce, and tomato. And a bag of chips and a cookie. Is that okay?"

Dalton bit his lip and nodded, afraid to say anything for fear of crying.

"It's okay, honey," she said softly. "You're always welcome here."

Dalton turned and started walking out of the kitchen. "We need to get to school," he muttered.

"Of course." Kate grabbed her purse. "Let me drive you both to school. Dalton, your bike is safe leaving it here for the day, and I'll come pick you both up this afternoon, okay?"

Dalton nodded, not saying another word.

"Thanks, Mom," Jason said, grabbing his backpack and the two lunches. He handed one to Dalton. "Here's yours. C'mon, let's get in the car."

***

Dalton glanced at Jason as they sat together at lunch eating their sandwiches. "Why is your mom so nice to me?"

Jason shrugged. "She's a good mom. And she likes you. Aren't all moms nice? Was your mom nice when she was alive?"

Dalton thought for a moment. "I guess. But she was pretty quiet. I don't remember her that well." He took a bite of his sandwich. "I guess my dad was the loud one. He yelled a lot about everything. And now he's the only one."

"I'm sorry. I know your dad is not very nice to you."

"Don't all dads hit their kids? Aren't they all like that?"

Jason shook his head. "No, mine is not like that. I don't think he ever hit me. My dad takes me to the park and we play ball, and we play games together and do fun stuff. He's a good dad."

Dalton stared at his friend for a few moments. "That must be nice," he said, his voice barely audible.

***

One week later, Dalton sat at the small desk upstairs in his bedroom and stared at his homework, drumming his pencil on the desk. He read the math question again and tried to figure out …

Shouting suddenly interrupted his concentration and he stared at his closed bedroom door, trying to listen to what was happening downstairs. A strange male voice was yelling. His dad shouted back. More yelling.

Dalton covered his ears. He hated when his dad flew into a rage. That's when he became the most violent. He felt his body shake as he knew what would come next. His dad would come storming upstairs, burst into his bedroom, grab him, and ... Bile rose in his throat. He hated this. He was so tired of being beaten up.

The shouting downstairs stopped. Were they done? Then a shot rang out. What was that? Did one of them shoot the other? And if so, which one? Terror gripped him. Would one of them come up and shoot him too? His hands were cold and shaking. What was happening down there?

He didn't hear any footsteps, and there were no more shouts. Was the other guy still here? It sounded quiet, but he didn't trust it.

Trembling, he stayed in his room another hour. Finally, he tiptoed to his bedroom door, slowly opened it, and peeked out. Silence. No one was there.

Stealthily going down the stairs, he kept listening for any threat. Nothing. Reaching the bottom, he turned and glanced in the living room.

He gasped and took a step back.

A man's body lay on the floor, face down, a pool of blood spreading out from under him.

Dalton felt his eyes widen. Was that ...? He stepped closer. *No! Dad ...*

68

"Dad?" he called out meekly.

No response.

Was he dead? What was he supposed to do? Was he supposed to call someone? He didn't want to call the cops—what if they took him away? He had no idea what to do. Where should he go? Who could help him?

Feeling dizzy and weak, he looked around for something to lean on. His legs buckled, and he collapsed onto the floor.

After sitting there a few minutes feeling dazed, a horrible thought hit him. All those times after he had been beaten by this man and he wished his father were dead ... had he caused this? Had his thoughts caused his father's death? Was this his fault?

A black wave of nausea overwhelmed him, and he leaned forward and gagged, then broke out in a sweat. He had to get out of there.

Grabbing his key, he ran out to his bicycle. There was only one place he could think of to go. His friend's house.

Alternating feelings of terror, shock, fear, and emptiness overwhelmed him as he rode his bike to Jason's house while trying to focus on the road.

Shaking, gulping down nausea, and not even knowing what to say, he rang their bell.

Jason's mom answered the door, took a look at him, and quickly ushered him in. She had him sit in the den and brought him a glass of water. Then she sat next to him and asked him what happened.

Through choking sobs, Dalton sputtered out the story. Not caring anymore, overcome with grief and shock, he held nothing back. He shared stories of the beatings, the rage, and the feeling that he didn't matter to anyone. "I don't know what to do. I didn't know where else to go. I'm sorry." Then, spent and exhausted, he put his head in his hands and cried quietly.

When he finally looked up, he saw Kate watching him, tears running down her cheeks. She reached forward and squeezed his hand. "You matter to me." Then she stood up. "Stay here tonight. Let me take care of a few things. You just relax. Don't worry about anything. You're safe here."

When she returned, she sat down quietly. "Have you eaten?"

He shook his head. "I can't even remember. I don't know. I can't eat now."

She talked with him in gentle tones a few more minutes, and then Jason joined them. An hour later, she walked down the hall and returned a few minutes later with a pillow and a blanket. "You can sleep here for now. We'll talk more in the morning, okay? For now, try and get some sleep."

***

Nightmares haunted Dalton's dreams, and he kept waking up not sure where he was or what was happening. Groggy, he looked around each time, then remembered bits and pieces of shouting, rage, a gunshot, a body ... Then he dozed off again, only to wake up a short time later, shaking. By morning, he was exhausted and miserable, his eyes burning and puffy.

The smell of bacon and eggs roused him, and he could hear noises coming from the kitchen. Slowly sitting up, he looked around, confused and disoriented. Then he shuddered as the memory of his dad lying on the ground in a pool of blood hit him and overwhelmed him.

He took a deep breath and let it out slowly. What was he going to do now? He trudged into the kitchen and saw Jason's mom at the stove.

Kate turned to him and smiled. "I hope you got some sleep." She motioned to the kitchen table. "Sit, I have breakfast made for you." After waiting for Dalton to sit at the table, she continued. "Jason will be here any minute. I hope you like eggs and bacon."

Dalton looked up at her with red, swollen eyes. "I've never eaten breakfast like this at home."

Jason's mom gazed at him. "You haven't?"

Dalton shook his head and then shrugged. "No. My dad doesn't make me breakfast. I usually have cold cereal."

Jason entered the kitchen, his hair messy, and he sat at the table. "Did I hear my name? And that smells good. I'm starving!"

Kate placed a plate of hot eggs and bacon on the table in front of each of the boys. "Eat. And there's more if you want." She watched Dalton hesitate. "It's okay, really. I made plenty."

She placed glasses of orange juice on the table and then watched as the two boys hungrily ate their breakfast and chatted in between bites.

After they finished, she sat at the table with them. "Dalton, I have something I need to tell you."

He looked up at her, and she continued. "I called the cops last night. Your dad didn't make it." She paused a few moments. "They have taken care of things and removed your dad's body. I'm sorry." She took a deep breath. "They said we are now allowed back in. This afternoon, if you're up to it, I'd like to go back with you so you can pick up some of your things. Clothes, books, toys, pictures, anything you want. And then you can stay here with us."

Dalton looked at her and blinked. "I don't want to be in the way."

"Oh, honey, you're not in the way. I've seen how you ... I have wanted to help you for a long time. And now I can."

"Thank you, Mrs. Daniels," he answered softly.

"Please call me Kate." She reached forward and squeezed his hand. "Do you have any other family? Grandparents? Aunts or uncles? Anyone to call?"

Dalton shook his head. "No. There's no one. I don't know where to go or what to do. I'm sorry. I don't want to be a bother." He fidgeted with his fingers.

"You're not at all. We'll take care of everything." She paused a few moments and then continued. "For now, just relax. You're safe here. And you're welcome to stay here for as long as you need while we get everything figured out."

He nodded and stared at the floor. "What about Mr. Daniels?"

"Marty feels the same way I do. He cares about you a lot, believe me. And I assure you, he will never hit you. Ever. You are safe here. I promise."

***

One week later, Dalton sat at the kitchen table and took another bite of chocolate cream pie. "Thank you, Kate. I love this. This is my very favorite."

She smiled at him. "I know, honey. And I have some news for you."

"You do? What?" He looked at her expectantly.

"We spoke to a lawyer. He researched your family and did not find anyone who would be able to take you. So we have filled out an application and all the paperwork. We would like to officially adopt you and make you a permanent member of our family."

Dalton dropped his fork on his plate. "What? Are you serious?"

She squeezed his hand. "Yes. You have been in my heart for years and I already love you as my own son."

Dalton's voice was soft. "You mean this would be my home? You would be my mom?"

"Yes, honey. Would you like that?"

A strangled sob came from Dalton as he stared at her. "Are you sure you want me?"

A tear ran down Kate's cheek. "More than you could possibly know."

"I ... I ... " he choked out and could not go on.

Kate moved closer to him and hugged him. "Welcome home, Dalton."

~~~

FIRST STEPS OF RECOVERY

D**anielle grimaced in** pain and massaged her right thigh. It was aching again, even more than usual. Both legs ached, but the right one was worse today. She wondered if she would ever stop hurting.

Rage surged through her as her mind drifted back to the accident that had left her crippled. She had been crossing the street and was in the crosswalk when some guy who was high on something came barreling down the road, driving much too fast, and hit her. She had gone flying, and both legs were shattered, along with a fracture and dislocation of a vertebra in her lower back. If only she could take that day back and have walked somewhere else instead. But she couldn't. It happened. And she didn't want to lose herself in the depths of anger and self-pity. She needed to move forward and not dwell on the past.

When she had first come to the hospital, the doctors had said that she may never walk again. There was the possibility of being paralyzed from the waist down. But after lumbar spinal fusion surgery, and now with plates and pins in her legs, she was getting feeling and movement in her lower limbs again. She spent many days working through the pain, going to physical therapy, and learning to walk again. It was now time to let anger go and to heal.

And finally, it was time to be discharged. Today was the day. She couldn't wait to get out of the hospital but, at the same time, she did not feel ready. She felt safe and protected while in the hospital, and her stomach fluttered with nerves at the thought of being on her own. Was she ready to be independent yet? A lump rose in her throat. She had been dreaming of walking on the beach, but that dream now seemed distant.

"Hey, beautiful!" Miles strode into the hospital room, a big smile on his face, his light brown hair hanging over his forehead. "Today's the day. Ready to go?"

She smiled back at her boyfriend. "I think so. I can't wait to get out of here. But I'm nervous, Miles."

"I know, sweetheart." He placed a light kiss on her lips. "But you'll be fine. And I'll be here to help you every step of the way."

"I know. You've really helped me through all of this. I could not have done this without you."

"Hey, where do you want to go on your first day of freedom?"

Danielle's smile grew wider. "To the beach."

"Dani, there's a storm coming in." Miles' face got serious. "The beach is not the best idea today."

"I don't care. It's my first day out of this hospital, and I really want to go to the beach. Even if it's only for five minutes."

"Okay, sweetheart. The beach it is." He ran his fingers through his disheveled hair. "Ready?"

Danielle nodded and pointed to her small bag. "That's it. I'm ready."

A young woman in a scrub suit entered the room with a wheelchair. "Okay, dear, we have to take you down in a wheelchair, it's hospital regulations."

Danielle checked her back brace, then carefully eased into the chair and sighed. Even sitting in the wheelchair was awkward. How would she walk on the sand? But she was determined. This was all she had thought about for the past week—walking on the beach. Especially on her first day out.

After being wheeled out of the hospital and slowly shimmying into Miles' car, Danielle licked her lips. "I'm scared, Miles."

"Do you really still want to go to the beach?" He leaned into the car and pointed. "Look at the weather. The wind is really strong."

She looked through the windshield at the heavy, dark gray clouds overhead, and spoke softly. "Yes. I still want to go."

"Okay, the beach it is." He closed the passenger door, got in on the driver's side, and started the car. "You doing okay?"

Danielle nodded. "I think so. I really want this."

Miles reached over and squeezed her hand. "You got it."

Twenty minutes later, he parked the car in the empty lot next to the desolate beach. The entire area was deserted.

Danielle giggled. "It's beautiful."

"What?" Miles' gaze searched her face. "You can't be serious. Look at it out there! The storm is crazy! It would be hard to walk out there even if you were in great shape."

"I know," she whispered. "It's fresh and real and raw and exciting. Nothing like the hospital." She returned Miles' gaze. "I have to do this."

She put her hand on the car door and hesitated. What if she couldn't walk here on the soft sand? She wasn't sure she had the strength yet. This was probably a bad idea. She bit her lip and gazed out at the storm whipping the waves as whirlwinds of sand blew across the beach.

Miles reached out and touched her cheek. "You don't have to do this today."

"Yes, I do." She quickly wiped a tear that ran down her cheek. "I have to do this."

"I'm here for you, sweetheart. I believe in you."

Danielle looked up into his eyes. "Miles, I'm not sure I can."

"Sure you can. I know you, Dani. Let's go. Show me. I'll be with you."

She took in a deep breath. "You're right. I have to. If I don't do this today, I'll regret it. I don't care what the weather is. I won't let anything get in my way—not a hurricane, a tornado, or a downpour. Nothing will stop me. This is my day. My first day of freedom and recovery."

"I'm here. I will walk beside you no matter what."

"Okay, here I go." Danielle opened the car door and swung her legs out. The wind wrenched the door open and she gasped. She slowly stepped out of the car, grabbing for the door. Her hair whipped across her face and up in the air as she slammed the door shut. She squinted against the wind as tears formed in her eyes. It didn't matter. This was her time.

Miles ran to her side. "Dani, you got this. You will be fine." His fingers brushed her hair back. "You hear me?"

Danielle nodded, as tears ran down her cheeks.

She stepped off the pavement and took two steps forward in the sand, feeling the gale-force wind buffet her, almost knocking her over. She took a few more steps. A powerful gust of wind threw her off balance, and Miles grabbed her. Two more steps.

Fat drops of rain splattered down from the heavy, dark clouds. Danielle laughed, threw her arms out to the side and spun in a slow circle.

A brilliant flash of lightning split the sky.

Danielle glanced at Miles. "Okay, maybe it's time to go."

Miles nodded and helped her back to the car. Once inside, she turned to him. "Thank you. This really meant a lot to me. Even just a few steps."

He nodded. "I know. This was important to you."

"All those days in the hospital I dreamed of this day. My first day being free. The start of my independence and recovery." She wiped the raindrops off her face. "I feel on top of the world now. I know I'll be okay."

Miles looked at her, his eyes misty. "Dani, you'll be more than okay. You amaze me. You can do anything."

"Well, I don't know about that, but I know I'll walk again. And I feel great."

Another flash of lightning lit up the sky, and a powerful crash of thunder immediately followed. Rain pelted and splattered on the windshield in huge drops, making it hard to see.

"Okay," Danielle said with a laugh. "That was enough. I think it's time to go home."

"You got it," Miles said, driving out of the empty, wet parking lot and back onto the road. "You doing okay?"

Danielle sighed. "Yeah, I'm achy and sore, but I'm glad I did this." She leaned her head back on the headrest. "And now I'm exhausted and I can't wait to get home. I need to rest for a while. It's been a big day."

Miles nodded. "But you did it."

"Yeah, I did it. After all I've been through, I walked on the beach." Danielle smiled. "I am no longer a victim. Now my recovery can really begin. I am free."

~~~

ton

BUCKET OF LIFE

Squeezing pressure. Hard to breathe. My chest ached. My jaw hurt. Dizziness flooded through me and I felt weak. I stumbled to the phone and called 911. Didn't feel well. Nauseous. Felt awful. Could not take a deep breath. Shuffled to the front door and unlocked it. Lay down on the floor in front of the unlocked door and hoped they would get there in time. Darkness.

Surrounded by a flurry of activity. I was placed on a gurney. I felt a mask pressed to my face. I felt movement and heard sirens as the ambulance raced to the hospital. Felt hot and sweaty. Would I make it? Not sure I would survive. Darkness.

A room. Surrounded by doctors in blue scrub suits. I ached all over. Felt heavy. Something was horribly wrong.

"We're losing her again."

I floated up. Surrounded by brilliant white light. Warm and soothing.

"Clear!"

Who was talking? I looked down from the ceiling and watched my body bounce on the hospital bed. Doctors frantically moved and worked on my body. But I was up here above it all. That wasn't me anymore. I was light and free. No more pain.

The light softened and I was surrounded by dazzling yellow flowers. They were so beautiful. And butterflies—hundreds of them. Thousands. They were exquisite. What was this place? Where was I?

A figure approached. Familiar, but looked different. My mom! She looked like she used to look when she was younger.

"Mom!" I called out to her.

She approached, a smile on her face. "It's not your time."

"What? No, I like it here. I don't want to go back."

"We'll meet again, I promise. But there's something you still need to do down there."

"No, I'm done there. I want to be here with you."

Beautiful music surrounded me. Beethoven? Chopin? Mozart? I wasn't sure. But it was familiar and overpowering. I loved it.

My mom had something in her hand. "You have to go back and do something."

"No, don't make me go back."

"Here." She handed me something.

"What is this?" I looked at it. It was a small bucket.

"You'll know what to do."

"Huh?" I looked at the bucket—it was pink with yellow polka dots. What was this for?

"Clear!"

I bounced on the bed. I was so achy. Pain radiated throughout my body.

"She's back!"

"Jenna, can you hear me?"

Where was I? I tried to respond. My eyes wouldn't open. My mouth was dry.

"I see movement. She's responding now."

My eyes flew open. Doctors surrounded me, peering down at me.

"Jenna, can you hear me?"

I nodded. What happened to my dream? I remembered having such a nice dream. I couldn't quite remember it, but it was nice.

A mask was placed on my face and I relaxed. There was a flurry of activity. I was moved to another gurney and wheeled somewhere. I slept.

***

A month later, I sat at my kitchen table for lunch and sipped an iced tea. I had recovered from my heart attack, but that really scared me and left me feeling vulnerable. And recovery was slow—I still didn't feel great. I was alive, but I was not sure for what. Here I was, in my late sixties, retired, and no close friends. Why had I even survived? What good was my life?

I finished my sandwich and drank more iced tea. Feeling fatigued, I closed my eyes and let out a long sigh. It felt good to relax, even if I was still achy. Vague memories of a dream flitted through my mind, but I couldn't quite catch it. I remembered seeing my mom. It had seemed so real. And she had given me something. Something important. But I couldn't remember what it was.

I got up, placed the dirty dishes in the sink, and wandered aimlessly into the garage. Glancing around, everything seemed in place, except ... what was that? It looked like a few of my storage boxes had been moved. But I didn't remember moving them.

I moved closer. A pink handle of some sort stuck out next to one of the boxes. Something tickled in the back of my mind as I slowly reached forward and pulled on the handle. A pink bucket with yellow polka dots. What the ... I gasped as the memory flooded back. *The dream!* That's what my mom had given me in that dream! *Nooooo!*

How was that possible? I never had this object in real life. This was a dream object. It crossed over from the dream world into the real world. It made no sense. A shiver ran through me.

I looked inside the bucket. There was a folded piece of paper at the bottom—a note with writing on it. I cautiously pulled out the note, opened it, and read it.

Hartview Bridge. Today. 2:00 pm.

I felt my heartbeat quicken. My mouth went dry. What was this? I felt a vague pressure in the air. Was I having another heart attack? No, I felt okay. Just a vague overall pressure. I didn't know why, but I knew I had to be at the Hartview Bridge at 2:00. I glanced at my watch. I'd have to leave in ten minutes. I didn't want to be late for whatever it was.

I arrived at the bridge with five minutes to spare. I quickly scanned the area but didn't see anything. Then movement caught my eye, and I squinted and started walking closer. A young teenager, male, maybe fifteen or sixteen, walked to the middle of the bridge. I felt that pressure increase. I still didn't understand it, but I knew this young man was why I was here.

I quickened my steps and rushed forward. As I got closer, I could see that his hair was disheveled and his face was streaked with tears. Now twenty feet away, I could hear gasps and choking sobs coming from him.

He climbed up onto the first of three rungs that spanned the length of the bridge. I knew instantly that he intended to jump. I sprinted to him, and as he climbed up onto the second rung, I grabbed him around the waist and pulled him down.

He gasped and sputtered and spun around, looking at me. "What the hell? Leave me alone!"

"No, please don't jump. Please. Talk to me. Whatever it is, don't end your life. You're needed here."

He scowled and looked angry. "You don't know me. You don't know anything."

I nodded. He was right. I had no idea what his life was like. "Please just talk to me." I spoke softly. "My name is Jenna. What is your name?"

He hesitated. "Shawn," he whispered.

"Shawn, whatever you're dealing with—"

"No, you don't understand. I can't take it anymore. I'm tired of the bullying. I'm tired of getting beat up." His face contorted and he sobbed. "Everyone hates me and makes fun of me because I'm gay. But that's who I am. I can't—"

I squeezed his shoulder. "Actually, I do understand. My cousin is gay and I know what he's been through. And I'm bi." I hesitated and then went on. "Shawn, I promise you're safe with me." He sniffed and nodded. When he stayed and didn't run away, I continued. "Can I buy you lunch? Please? Let's talk."

He nodded and began sobbing again. I reached for him and hugged him. I held onto him. After a couple minutes, I felt his body relax and I felt him cling to me. My heart broke for him. As we walked to my car and I took him to lunch, the pressure around me eased, and I knew that's what I was here for. And I also knew I was the right person to help him.

***

A couple weeks later, I went into the garage to get a bottle of water. I felt a familiar pressure building. It occurred to me that I had not looked in that bucket in a while. I picked up the pink pail with the yellow polka dots and looked inside. Another note was at the bottom. How was this possible?

I picked up the note and read it.

439 Magnolia Blvd. Today. 10:30 am.

Chills ran up my spine. I felt gripped by that same pressure as it increased. I knew I had to be there. And I had to leave right away.

Parking my car two houses away from that address, I walked toward the building. It was a modest, two-story, gray house with white shutters and white trim. What was I doing here? I walked closer to the house. The lawn had been recently mown, and the hedges were neatly trimmed.

Shouts from the second story drew my attention. Looking up, I saw smoke billowing out of one of the windows. A woman, holding a baby, leaned out the window as flames shot out behind her. She wailed and looked around frantically. "Help!" she called out. "Is anyone there?" She screamed. "I'm not going to make it." Flames licked the wall around her. "I'm sorry, my baby. Please survive." She threw the baby out the window, trying to aim for some shrubbery.

I saw the baby flying through the air, screeching, its little arms flailing. I rushed forward toward the baby and caught him as he fell into my arms. I held him and rocked him as I heard sirens racing toward us. I glanced up and saw the woman straddling the window, ready to jump. She looked toward the sound of the fire engines and then saw me holding her precious baby. I rocked her sweet baby and talked to him as his mother's heart-wrenching sobs filled the air. Within moments, firefighters rushed over with ladders and they climbed up to rescue the woman.

A few minutes later, I handed her the sweet baby, who was now cooing and reaching for his mama.

The pressure around me eased, and I knew I was done. I got back in my car and headed home.

***

Confusion settled around me. Who was putting the notes in that bucket? Why was I chosen for this? How long would this go on? But I received no answers.

Later that week, I felt the familiar pressure building again, and I ran to the garage and looked in the pink bucket. Sure enough, there was a note in there.

Lake Granada. South side. Today. 3:00 pm.

My gut knotted up. What was going on? Why me? I didn't understand any of it. But I also knew I had to be there.

Parking my Honda in the parking lot by the lake, I checked the sign to make sure I was at the south end of the lake. I was. I got out of the car and looked around at the peaceful setting. Graceful sycamore and maple trees surrounded the lake. A cool fresh breeze blew off the water and washed over me as I walked toward the lake.

I thought I heard something. The pressure around me intensified. Again I heard a sound. Whimpering. Coming from the lake. I ran to the edge. Something was in the water—a small dog struggling to stay afloat. I could tell it was fatigued and could not make it to shore. I quickly took off my shoes and socks and ran into the cold water. The dog went under, then came back up, its snout barely breaking the surface. I swam as fast as I could. The dog saw me coming and tried to hold on, but I could see it was losing strength. It went under again just as I reached it. I quickly grabbed the furry brown dog and pulled him out of the water and held him to me. He clung to me as best he could, panting, making small whimpering noises.

Holding the poor dog in one hand I slowly made my way through the water to the shore. Breathing heavily and climbing out onto the small sandy area, I looked at the dog. I was fatigued myself, and I knew the dog would not have lasted much longer.

Grabbing an old towel from the back of my car, I sat down in a grassy area and examined the dog as I dried him with the towel. He looked like a terrier mix to me, exhausted but okay. I sat with him a few more minutes, drying him and comforting him. He licked my face. He was a sweet dog and looked like he had been well cared for. He must have gotten lost. He had a collar and a tag, and I called the number listed. The owner answered. Yes, he had lost his dog and had been frantic, trying to find him.

We made arrangements to meet, and I felt the pressure ease.

***

I hoped that would be all I was requested to do. I did not want to be in this position. I was tired and confused and still did not understand any of it.

The next week, I felt that familiar pressure building again. Reluctantly, I went into the garage and looked in the pink bucket with the yellow polka dots. Another note.

Market St. and Fourth Ave. SW corner. Today. 11:00 am.

Did I want to do this? I had to. I had no choice—it was compelling. The pressure was building, and I knew I needed to be there.

I parked my Honda down the street and walked to that corner. I didn't see anything unusual, and I felt uncomfortable standing there just waiting for something to happen.

The pressure increased. Traffic was busy at that intersection, but not busier than usual. The light turned green, and I saw an older man waiting to cross the street as he watched the light but not the cars. A van was barreling down the street, and it was clear that it was not going to stop—it was going to run the red light. The man stepped off the curb, into the path of the van.

I jumped forward, grabbing the man's arm and pulling him back onto the curb. "Hey—" he yelled as he fell back onto me and we both crashed to the sidewalk. "What the hell—"

The van rushed past us, the wind and dust kicking up behind it and blowing over us. We both stared after the van. "It would have hit you," I said softly.

The old man looked at me. "I just wanted to get a newspaper," he muttered.

"Are you okay?"

He nodded and I helped him get up. "Thank you, miss." He ran his fingers through his thinning hair. "Thank you."

I felt the pressure ease, and I patted him on the back. Before I left, I warned him to look both ways at the traffic before he stepped off the curb, and to be safe.

***

There were no more notes for a couple weeks, and then it started again. A few times each month I went on assignments, following the instructions on each note as it appeared. As much as it was rewarding to help others, it was also a bit unnerving. It was hard to wrap my head around it, and I never felt worthy of being in that position.

After about six months, the bucket remained empty for a few weeks. I wondered if it was over. Was I done? Who was sending the notes anyway? And how? It was all baffling and also exhausting. And I still did not understand any of it or why it was happening. And why me? Was I supposed to learn something? Make amends for something? I had no idea.

Then I felt the pressure build again. I made my way into the garage to the familiar bucket and pulled out the note.

Your living room. Today. 8:00 pm.

Huh? What or who would need my help in my own living room? But I knew I would honor the call. At 7:30, I sat on the couch in my living room. All was quiet. I turned on the TV and watched the news. Almost 8:00. The pressure increased. But no one else was there.

The pressure suddenly intensified. My heart pounded. My heart felt like it was exploding in my chest. What was this? My jaw ached. *No!* Nausea overwhelmed me and I broke out in a sweat. I ran for the phone. My legs gave way and I collapsed after a few steps. I could not reach the phone. It was hard to breathe. My vision grew black.

The room now flooded with bright light.

My mom was here again! "Mom!"

She smiled and opened her arms to greet me. "Hi, honey."

I felt light and free. Brilliant yellow flowers were everywhere. Butterflies filled the air. A sweet, delicate fragrance washed over me.

I remembered that I had questions and needed answers. "Mom, how did the pink bucket appear in physical form? And why did I have to do all that? And why me?"

She laughed and glowed with love. "It will all become clear as you meet with your guide. That will happen shortly. Then you will understand all of it."

"Okay." That made sense and satisfied me for now. I smiled back at her as the butterflies danced around us. "Can I stay here this time?"

She nodded, as warmth and light radiated from her. "Yes, you can stay. Welcome home, honey."

I was floating and it was intoxicating. Sparkles of glittering light flowed endlessly around me. That beautiful music permeated the air. A powerful sense of love enveloped me. I couldn't help laughing as joy bubbled up within me.

The answers to my questions could wait. It was all okay.

I was home.

~~~

INNER LIGHTS

Jackie stared at her father. She hated him when he got like this.

He glared at her. "You're stupid," he shouted, his face contorted with rage. "What the hell are you gonna do with dancing? You can't make a living with that. That is a terrible idea! You never do anything right—that's why you're such a failure. Look at what you want to do with your life! Do you ever listen to anything I tell you? You're a horrible daughter, and you'll never amount to anything. Look at yourself!" Spittle flew from his lips as he raged at her. "Why can't you do something smart for once?"

Without saying a word, Jackie turned, ran up the stairs, and rushed to her room. She shut the bedroom door and then collapsed on her bed, tears running down her face. Pain and anger built inside her until she doubled over, clutching her belly. She couldn't live like this anymore.

She used to yell back at him when he got like that, but she quickly realized that only made it worse. Over the years, she had learned to keep her mouth shut. But it was too much. She hated him and she hated living there. And she hated herself too.

Maybe there really *was* something wrong with her. Maybe her father was right. Maybe she would never be smart enough or make the right choices or do anything well. And now that her boyfriend had left her the previous week for another girl—a prettier one—her world crashed in on her.

Her dad screaming at her now was more than she could deal with, and it pushed her over the edge. She couldn't handle any of this. She would never be good enough. And it was time she realized it. Her sobs made her choke and cough, and she gasped for air, holding onto the edge of her bed.

She stood up and shuffled to the mirror over her dresser, looking at her image. She hated how she looked. Her eyes were red and puffy, and she looked miserable. Ugly. All she could see were her many flaws—everything she hated about herself.

After coughing a few more times, she turned away from the mirror and choked back another sob. She had to get out of there. Life wasn't even worth living anymore.

Jackie grabbed her purse and a sweatshirt, and she paused at her bedroom door, listening. No sound reached her—it was silent in the house. Where was her father? Slowly opening the door a crack, she peered out. Empty. She hoped she wouldn't run into him.

She gently closed the bedroom door behind her, quietly ran down the stairs, and ran out the front door. Blindly, she raced down the street, down another, and out of the neighborhood, heading toward the woods. Maybe she could find some peace there. Or maybe she would just end it all.

Stomping down the dirt path, she was oblivious to the trees and dense green foliage surrounding her, as anger, humiliation, and depression fought inside her. What could she do? Where could she go? She hated herself and her life. It was too much for her.

Kicking at the dirt and rocks as she walked, a heavy sense of despair overtook her. Holding the purse and sweatshirt close to her, she took shallow breaths and swallowed hard. Something had to change. She didn't even want to be alive anymore.

Another half mile down the path, she suddenly stopped. What was that? The entrance to a dark cave in a small hillock stared back at her. She didn't remember ever seeing that before. It seemed to beckon to her, and she felt herself drawn to it. Maybe that was the answer—a dark cave to oblivion. A place to hide and leave her life behind. At least for now.

After a brief pause, she trudged toward the cave entrance. Goosebumps rose on her arms. What was in there? Was it safe? She didn't care. It didn't even matter anymore.

She hesitated for a few moments and then took a few steps forward. She knew she was giving up. She no longer cared what happened, and she slowly entered the cave.

The intense darkness closed in on her, almost suffocating her. Slightly dizzy, she felt her way along one rocky wall, and as her eyes adjusted, she began to see the dirt floor and large rocks forming the walls of the cave. She walked farther in, and the light dimmed. The cold dampness of the cave enveloped her and she shivered.

Tired and spent, her eyes burning, she sat down on the cold dirt floor near the wall and sighed. No longer caring about anything, she took a deep breath and let it out slowly. If her life ended here, that was fine with her. Shivering again, she rubbed her arms and then put on her sweatshirt.

Exhaustion overtook her, and she lay down on the cave floor, placing her purse under her head as a pillow. Feeling dizzy, she didn't care if she ever woke up. She started drifting off and finally dozed.

An hour later, Jackie suddenly jerked awake and abruptly sat up. Terror gripped her—where was she? She remembered a strange dream about tiny points of light that spoke to her. She shook her head to clear it and rubbed her eyes. She peered into the darkness, trying to see.

As she looked around, something seemed to move by her. What was that? A small flash of light zipped by. A firefly? No—there were more of them. Just like the ones in her dream! At least four or five points of light now surrounded her, swirling and pulsing. *What were those?*

Whispers filled the cave and her skin prickled. A voice echoed somewhere, bouncing off the walls of the cave.

We are here to help you, a voice echoed.

She looked around, seeing nothing other than the points of light. "Who are you?" she asked, her voice raspy.

We can help you, the voice stated.

She leaned against the wall, clutching her purse and holding it tightly, not sure what was happening.

We see you struggling. We can offer you one wish to help you.

"One wish? I'm not sure I understand."

We will grant you one wish—whatever you wish for, any one thing, you will have.

Was this for real? Just in case it was, she thought for a few moments. What should she ask for? What could help her? She briefly thought about asking for money, pretty clothes, a better body, nicer hair, or even a pizza. Maybe a different father.

But after mulling it over, she shook her head, dismissing those ideas. Those were all things she hoped would make her life better, but she quickly realized they wouldn't. All of those were on the outside, and she was still miserable on the inside. What would make her happy? What should she ask for?

After thinking it over for a few more minutes, she licked her dry lips. "Okay, I've decided," she finally whispered to the air.

What is your wish?

A small smile played on her lips. "I wish to be happy."

The lights swirled and flew around her and then hovered in front of her. The whispering voice spoke one word: *Done.*

She looked around. "But I don't feel any different."

Look in a mirror, the voice said.

Feeling confused, she opened her purse and took out a small mirror. This was absurd. She held up the mirror in the dim light. At first it was hard to see, but then the image seemed to lighten, and her face became visible.

It was her own face, but it somehow looked and seemed different. Instead of seeing her flaws and everything she hated, she now saw something else reflected back to her.

As she stared at her image, she saw someone warm and loving looking back at her. Was that her? She peered at her image more intently.

Something was shifting, and she seemed to see inside herself at a deeper level. A sense of her inner self, an inner beauty. She saw her gentleness, her compassion, her kindness. She saw how she cared about others. She saw her sensitivity which helped her be a sweeter and kinder person. She saw the loving way she treated others. She saw her gracefulness and fluidity as she danced. She saw an inner beauty that was mesmerizing and overwhelming. And as she gazed at her image, a rush of warmth flooded over her.

Why was she seeing this? What happened? She wasn't sure. But something inside had definitely shifted. It was still her, but a part of her had opened. A part she had not really seen before.

She knew it no longer mattered what her father did or said. Whatever he did reflected on him, not her. Somehow she now felt free. She would follow her own heart and what she loved. She knew what was important to her. Dancing brought her joy, and that's what she would pursue. And she would not let anything stand in her way.

And another boyfriend? She would find someone who loved her exactly as she was. She would not accept anything less. Another powerful wave of intense warmth moved through her, and she felt a sense of inner strength and determination. And something new—a growing feeling of self-love.

She felt her lips curve up into a smile. She looked around to thank the points of light, but they were no longer visible. Where did they go? Were they ever really there?

She wasn't sure. But she knew one thing. For the first time in a very long time, she was happy.

~~~

ENDLESS CONNECTION

J oyce stood there, staring into the open grave. A layer of dirt, thrown on there by the shovelful, now lay on top of the casket. How could her brother Jake have died so young? It wasn't fair.

Glancing away and focusing on a nearby tree, she sucked in a breath and shuddered. Then she looked back into the grave as tears ran down her face. Anguish, regret, and grief overwhelmed her, and she covered her face with her hands. How could she live without him? Jake was more than her brother—he was her twin and her best friend. They were bonded together. He should still be here. She shook her head as grief engulfed her. It made no sense.

Choking, her breath ragged, she left the cemetery and drove to a nearby park. After parking the car, she walked along the dirt path that circled the lake. At one end, a red bench sat nestled in the trees. Exhausted and overwhelmed, she settled on the bench and gazed out over the clear, blue lake.

"Why, God? Why?" She looked up at the sky, but she knew there was no answer.

Her thoughts drifted back to the last time she had seen him, just a few short days ago. He was wearing that red and black flannel shirt that he loved, a silly, goofy smile on his face, his light brown hair hanging over his forehead. The image brought a sad smile to her face. She loved his goofiness—he could make her laugh no matter what. And she loved him in that shirt. In fact, she insisted that he be buried in that shirt. It suited him and was the way she would always remember him.

He was her twin in many ways. They were like one person so much of the time. They could read each other's thoughts, finish each other's sentences, and just look at each other and know what the other was thinking. It was like they had a psychic connection. And now ... now her soul yearned for that connection, but he wasn't there. Her heart felt crushed. Empty. He was her other half, and she kept expecting him to be right there. How was she supposed to survive without him?

She took a deep breath, listening to the sounds of the gentle waves on the lake and the leaves rustling above her in the trees. Something drifted down in her line of vision—two beautiful, soft feathers. She held out her cupped hand and caught one of them, while the other fluttered to the ground. She looked at the feather in her hand—it was silky and red and black. "Jake? Is that you? Did you send this to me?" Silence answered her. She could only hear the soft rippling of the lake and the rustling of leaves.

Looking down at the dirt near her feet, she saw the other red and black feather. She smiled. It had to be Jake. Two feathers for the two of them. Bending forward, as she reached for the feather, a spot of color caught her attention. Immediately under the feather was a small, torn corner of a blanket. Soft fleece in red and black. Too much to be a coincidence.

She picked up the second feather and the fleece. "Jake? I know it's you. But what are you telling me?" The corner of the blanket felt soft and comforting. It felt like peace. Her smile widened. Was he telling her he made it and he's now comfortable and at peace? She hoped so, and it felt right.

Letting out a long breath, she whispered to the air, "Thank you, Jake. I hope you're okay."

A soft whisper of wind gently caressed her hand, causing the two feathers to dance in her palm and then settle down.

She shook her head. The yearning for Jake was too strong—she must be imagining things. Her gaze drifted out over the lake one last time as she started to get up. Pushing herself up from the red bench, she stood and gazed at the two feathers and the piece of fleece in her hand. Something fluttered under the fleece—what was that? A thin piece of paper peeked out.

She picked up the small piece of paper and read the words printed on it.

I am home. I am at peace. I am with you.

She convulsed into sobs and then stuffed the feathers, the fleece, and the note into her pocket. There was no mistaking the message or who it was from. But how was that possible? She knew they had a strong, psychic connection, but could he do this?

"Thank you, Jake. I love you," she whispered to the air.

She started down the path toward her car. As she walked, a sweet woman's voice, singing a lullaby, drifted through the air and grew louder. As she walked farther down the path and got closer to the sweet voice, a young woman pushing a baby stroller came into view, and the young woman was gently singing to her baby.

Suddenly embarrassed, the lady blushed and stopped singing. Then she smiled at Joyce. "It's a beautiful, magical day, isn't it?"

Joyce stared at her for a moment, then quickly collected herself. "Yes, yes, absolutely. Beautiful and magical. Definitely."

She smiled at the lady and then walked by, hearing the woman begin singing the lullaby again. Joyce turned around to glance at the woman, but no one was there. The path was empty.

It made no sense. None of it made sense.

But Jake had sent her a clear message. The scent of his aftershave washed over her, and she could feel his warmth.

Yes, a beautiful and magical day indeed.

He was still with her. A connection that was truly endless.

~~~

HIDE AND SEEK

B enjie kept his eyes covered as he sang out. "... 6 ... 7 ... 8 ... 9 ... 10. Ready or not, here I come!" He dropped his hands and opened his eyes, taking in the back yard. His eyes roamed over the swing set, the picnic table, the big oak tree with the tree house, and a few smaller trees. But no Stevie. Where did he go?

Benjie knew he didn't hear Stevie climb the ladder to the tree house, but maybe he'd check anyway. He ran to the oak tree and climbed up the ladder. At the top, he leaned forward and peeked into the small, square, wooden room. A few coloring books, a box of crayons, and two juice boxes. But no Stevie.

He climbed back down. Where did his friend go? He ran around the back yard. "Stevie?" No answer.

A creaking sound made him turn toward the back of the yard. The gate was open. Did Stevie leave and go into the woods?

He knew they weren't supposed to leave the yard, as they were only six years old, but maybe that's where his friend went. He glanced back at the house. No one was visible. He knew his mom was inside making dinner. He wouldn't be gone long. A quick look and then he'd be back.

Benjie pushed open the squeaky gate and walked into the wild brush that grew up above his knees. Was it safe out here? He felt a little nervous. He had never been back here by himself. But he wouldn't go far.

"Stevie?" He looked at the tall trees. Maybe his friend was just a little farther in, behind one of the trees. "Hey, Stevie, answer me."

He nervously glanced behind him. He wasn't too far from home. He'd be okay. He'd find Stevie, they'd laugh, and then they'd go home.

He walked farther into the woods. A path became visible on his left. Maybe he'd follow the path for a bit. Maybe that's where Stevie went.

Benjie walked for a while, looking at the trees and listening to the chirping birds. A sudden cold wind cut through his thin t-shirt and he shivered. How far had he walked? Where was he?

He turned in a circle. He was on a path surrounded by tall trees and thick underbrush. How long had he been walking? He felt cold and hungry. His mom would be mad at him. Leaves rustled behind him and he jumped. He heard a thump. What was that?

Shivering with fear and the cold, he ran off the path and hid behind a tree. Silence settled around him, but his belly churned with fear. His hands shook. Panic rose in his chest and he tried not to cry. Where was he? Which way was home? He wasn't even sure which way he had been walking anymore.

He sat down in the dirt near a bush covered in thick leaves and shivered. Looking up, he saw the sky getting dark. How would he get home?

"Mommy?" he called out into the trees. He started to cry and wiped his nose with the back of his hand. Then he broke down in choking sobs.

Footsteps and men's voices startled him. What if they were bad guys? What if they killed him? His mom would never find him.

The heavy panting of an animal filled the air, and he heard the pounding of running paws on the ground. Benjie gasped and pulled in closer under the leafy bush. *No!*

The men's voices got closer. "Abby!" a man's voice called out.

"There she is," another voice said.

Benjie's eyes grew wide as the animal crashed through the trees and stopped next to him. A large German Shepherd sat down in front of him and barked. "Woof!"

"Good girl, Abby!" Two policemen stepped off the trail and stood next to the dog.

One of the cops peeked under the bush. "Are you Benjie?" he asked.

Benjie nodded and wiped tears off his cheeks.

"Benjie, we're cops, and we're here to help you get back home. I'm Sam, and that's Mike." The boy stared back at them, shaking. "Your mom called us. She's really worried about you."

Benjie sniffed and turned to look at the German Shepherd.

Sam kneeled down next to Benjie. "And I see you've met Abby." He stroked the dog's fur. "This is Officer Abigail, our K-9 officer who helped find you." He looked at the dog. "Good girl, Abby," he added and pulled a dog biscuit out of his pocket, holding it out to the pooch. Abby wagged her tail and took the treat, chewing noisily.

Sam looked back at the boy. "Are you okay? Are you hurt?"

Benjie's eyes met Sam's, and he shook his head. "I'm okay," he whispered. "I'm cold."

Sam spoke softly. "Let's get you home. Can you get up okay? Can you walk?"

Benjie nodded and stood up, brushing dirt and leaves off his dungarees. "Is my mom mad at me?"

"She's worried about you. We're gonna call in and let your mom know we found you and that you're safe, so she won't worry anymore. Then we'll take you home. Okay?"

***

Benjie ran up the steps to the front porch of his home and rushed into his mother's arms, crying. "I'm sorry, Mommy," he choked out.

She scooped him up and hugged him tightly, rocking back and forth. "It's okay, pumpkin. I'm glad you're home and you're safe." She kissed his head, breathing in his scent. "Where were you?"

"Out in the woods."

"You know you're not supposed to leave the yard."

"I ... I know," he stammered. "I was looking for Stevie and couldn't find him. Where was he?"

"Stevie was hiding behind a trash can at the side of the house. Then he got worried when you didn't find him, and he came inside and got me. We searched the yard, found the back gate open, and I called the police."

Benjie sniffed. "Their dog Abby found me. She's a good dog."

His mother turned to the officers who were waiting patiently on the porch. "Thank you, officers. I really appreciate all your help."

"Our pleasure, ma'am. We're glad this one had a happy ending."

"Me too." Her voice caught in her throat. "Oh God, me too."

The officers and the K-9 turned and walked to their squad car. Benjie looked up at his mom. "Mommy?"

"Yes, pumpkin?"

"I like Abby. Can we get a dog?"

His mom laughed. "That's not a bad idea. A dog might help keep you safe." She kissed Benjie's cheek. "Are you hungry? Let's go in and have dinner."

"Okay. I'd really like a dog. And I know what I want to be when I grow up."

"What, pumpkin?"

"A policeman. Just like those nice men. And I'll have a big dog just like Abby."

"That sounds nice. Now go wash your hands for dinner and we can talk about it, okay?"

~~~

HEAVEN LEVEL ONE

Colton rushed into the crosswalk, his mind running in a million directions. Having been fired from where he worked the week before, he needed to update his résumé and find a new job. And his girlfriend had just dumped him that morning. It was not a good day.

Shaking his head, anxiety and distress flooding him, he hurried across the street. Halfway through the crosswalk, a pickup truck coming from his right sped through the red light. He barely heard the squeal of tires and suddenly felt himself fly into the air.

Shocked, he opened his eyes. He was in a room that was all white. White floor, white walls, white ceiling, and white benches. Where was this? What happened?

As he looked around, he noticed other people sitting on some of the benches. Most people were elderly, but a few people were younger. Some looked bored or tired, and some looked shocked or confused.

A tall man with white curly hair entered the room and stood at the front. "Attention, everyone. May I please have your attention." He waited for a few moments as people turned to look at him. "Welcome to the processing room at Level One. My name is Vincent. We will be scheduling all of you shortly, so please be patient for a little while longer."

"Excuse me," a young man with bright red hair called out from the left side of the room. "Where are we? What is this room? Processing room for what?"

"Oh, I'm sorry. For those who don't know, you have recently passed away, and—"

"What?" the redheaded man asked. "We died? I'm dead?"

"Yes. All of you have died, but as you can see, your spirit lives on. So technically, your body died, but you are still very much alive. So, as I was saying, before you can—"

An older gray-haired woman raised her hand and started speaking right away, interrupting him. "Wait. I thought we'd be met by family members who passed before us."

Vincent sighed but stayed calm. "Yes, yes, they are waiting for you. After my announcements explaining how this works, you will be able to see your friends and family who have arrived here before you. Now before you can move forward into Heaven Level Two, you must first go through orientation here in Level One and successfully complete four classes."

He looked around the room, cleared his throat, and continued. "The first class is Review, which is a review of your previous life, where you will examine the life you just left and see how much you have helped or hurt others and what you have learned. This class is important and will determine how fast you can move through all the levels."

He checked his notes and then looked up. "The second class is Manifesting. In this class you will understand how manifesting works and you will learn to manifest what you want instantly. That is a fun class—everyone likes that one, and it's a skill you will need to master."

He sipped some water. "The third class is Wisdom, where you will learn to access the wisdom of the universe and let go of your own ego. This is an important class and will help you a lot as you progress to the other levels."

He looked around and made sure everyone was paying attention. "The fourth class, once you have finished the first three, is Guiding, where you will be assigned a person currently on Earth who you will learn to guide. Your job will be, for a limited time, helping them navigate the various issues and difficulties that come up in that person's life. Your own spirit mentor here will help match you to the right person for you and will help guide you through this."

After looking at everyone in the room, he continued. "After you successfully complete the first four classes, it will be determined who moves on to Level Two and who will return to Earth in a new incarnation. For those who will return to Earth, there is one additional class, Preparation, which you will need to take. For those who move on to Level Two, you will not take this last class, as your Level One will be complete."

He glanced at his notes again and then continued. "However, for those of you who will be returning to Earth in a new incarnation, and you will take this class to prepare for your return. You will be guided by a spirit mentor one-on-one, who will help you understand what it is you need to learn in a new life, so that you would be born into the right family, culture, location, religion, race, gender, etc. All of the variables will be reviewed and chosen to best help you progress and evolve."

He put his notes down. "Please note that if you do not successfully complete these classes on Level One, you will be required to take them again until you do complete them successfully. If you cause any problems or refuse to take them or if you skip any classes, you will be sent to detention."

A thin white-haired man spoke up, his voice sounding confused. "Detention?"

"Yes, we take things very seriously here. Being a spirit is not all fun and games. There is a lot to learn, and it is important that you learn it well. You will be assigned a guide or mentor to help you progress through the classes and beyond." He paused. "Are there any more questions?"

A small girl with brown curls spoke up. "When can we see our family?"

Vincent glanced at his watch. "We will take a break now for one hour. You are free to visit with your friends and family through that door." He pointed to the side. "Please make sure you are back here in one hour to attend your first class. Don't be late."

Colton watched as most of the people stood up and ran for the exit door that was now lit up with a red exit sign. He slowly got up and followed the group out. Would there be anyone here for him? The only ones he personally knew who had passed before him were his grandparents and one childhood friend.

As he stepped through the doorway, cool fresh air washed over him, and he looked around in awe. Surrounding him was a huge meadow of green grass with bushes, flowers in vivid colors, magnificent leafy trees, and a few wooden park benches. Water from a tall waterfall thundered from a cliff high above the trees.

A middle-aged couple approached him. After a moment, he recognized them—his grandparents! But they looked young and strong. "Welcome," they said, kissing him on the cheek.

"Grandma! Grandpa!" He smiled and hugged them. "It's so good to see you!"

Turning to his left, he noticed someone familiar approaching. "Colton! Hey, buddy!"

He suddenly recognized his childhood friend, Julian, who had passed away years ago. "Julian, is that you?"

Julian laughed. "It's me all right. Let's get out of here and have some fun."

"I can't. I only have one hour, then I need to take some classes, and—"

"Forget the classes, man. You know all that stuff. You don't need that."

"Yes, I do. If I skip any, I'll be sent to detention."

"Nah, do you know what detention is?" Julian let out a loud laugh. "It's just meditation. You don't need that. Let's have some fun."

"But I don't want to—"

Julian grabbed his arm and pulled him away from his grandparents. Colton waved helplessly at his grandparents who waved back. Julian dragged him toward a grove of trees. "We can do anything we want here. It's gonna be great! Want something to eat?"

"Well, now that you mention it, I am a little hungry."

Julian nodded. "Great! You want food? Then food it is. How about pizza, donuts, and beer? How does that sound?"

"Well, it sounds good, but I don't think—"

"Voilá!" Julian gestured to the side and a buffet table appeared in the grass, loaded with pizza, boxes of donuts, and bottles of beer. "You like?"

Colton stared at the table, his eyes wide with surprise. "How did you do that?" He reached for a slice of pizza and bit into the cheesy goodness. "Hey, this is really good."

"Easy! You'll learn about it in the manifesting class, but it's really simple. You can manifest anything you want by picturing it and focusing on it. We are pure energy here, and when your energy is directed toward it, it appears. Once you get the hang of it, you can manifest all kinds of stuff, including more complicated things like this—a buffet table with all the food you want."

"That's amazing! But I don't want to get fat." He patted his belly.

Julian laughed. "Fat? You can't get fat here—you don't even have a body anymore. You have the illusion of a body, but you are now pure energy. So you can eat all you want."

"Well, that's good." Colton chuckled nervously, reached for a second slice of pizza, and took a big bite. "This is better pizza than I had on Earth."

Julian chuckled. "Only the best for you, my friend!"

Colton gazed at the beautiful grounds. "This place is gorgeous."

"This is nothing. Remember when we took skiing lessons?" Colton nodded, and Julian continued. "Let's go skiing!"

"What?"

With a flash of light, Colton was surrounded by pine trees and snow. They stood at the top of a spectacular ski slope that wound its way down through the trees. Colton looked down and was surprised to find himself in ski clothes, complete with goggles, boots, poles, and skis. "Wow," he said, breathing in the cold, biting air.

"Last one down is a rotten egg," Julian called out as he took off laughing.

Colton raced after him, and they sped down the slope, dodging trees, wind blasting their faces. The gorgeous views and magnificent scenery sped past as they skied down the steep, snowy path. They finally arrived at the bottom almost at the same time.

Colton took off his goggles. "That was amazing! I loved that!"

"Pretty cool, huh?"

"Wow! I love this place! So tell me, what level are you at, that you can do all of this?"

Julian led him to a bench at the side of a snowdrift and sat down. "I'm at Level Four. I almost didn't make it because I tend to goof off too much, but now I'm there. And it's so cool."

"What's it like?"

"You can do and see things I never even knew were possible before. You can time travel. Well, actually, all time exists at the same moment, so it's just playing with the time continuum. It's really switching your focus to a specific spot in time and you're there, but it's all happening at once."

Colton shook his head. "I can't even understand that."

"It's okay, you will understand it when you get there." He shook snow off his boots. "And that's not all. There are different dimensions and alternate dimensions that exist at the same time. It's like tuning in to a different channel and focusing in a different realm."

"Can you take me there?"

"No, sorry, it's restricted. Those at lower levels don't have access. And you wouldn't be able to comprehend it anyway until you reach this level. It can be overwhelming."

Colton gazed around him at the snow. "Hey, can you fly?"

Julian laughed. "Fly? Sure—it's fun to fly. And you can also teleport anywhere. Want to see? Are you tired of the snow? Let's go to the beach."

A flash of light sparked the air, and heat washed over Colton as he looked around. Standing barefoot in the warm sand, he took in the vast deep blue ocean before him and the white-capped waves crashing onto the shore, foaming in the sand, and rushing up onto the beach. He took a deep breath, taking in the warm, humid, salty air. "Wow! This is amazing."

"Hey, you wanted to fly? Come on." Julian grabbed Colton's hand and they lifted up into the air. He glanced at Colton. "You okay?" Colton nodded, and Julian continued. "Good. Now just relax. Trust me."

They slowly glided forward over the water, a few feet above the choppy waves. Colton tensed up as fear moved through him, but he convinced himself to relax. Once he felt more calm, Julian took them higher, and they soared over the water as the wind rushed over them. They made a wide turn and raced back through the fresh air, flying above the water, and then gently landed back on the warm sand.

Julian looked at Colton. "How was that?"

"That was amazing." A bell sounded through the air. "What was that?"

Another flash of light, and they were back in the grassy field where they had first met. Julian looked around. "I think that's saying your hour is up and you need to go back to your orientation.

Colton nodded. "Well, it was good to see you." He looked around and saw his grandparents waving at him from a park bench. He waved back. He wished he could have visited with them longer.

Julian punched him in the arm. "Once you're out of your classes, we can visit any time. I have so much more to show you."

The bell sounded again. Colton glanced at Julian. "I need to get back to my classes."

"Ah, don't worry. It's just Level One. It's baby stuff. You can take the classes again later. Or maybe you can skip them—I'll vouch for you. We can have ice cream and listen to music. There's so much more to tell you! You're gonna love it here!"

"No, I can't be late. I need to—"

Colton found himself in the white room again. Vincent was the only other person there. Colton nervously glanced around. "Where is everyone?"

Vincent tapped his pen on the lectern and glared at him. "They are already in their first class." He paused for emphasis. "Where you should be, too."

"I'm sorry," Colton stammered. "I was—"

"No apologies here. Only action is accepted. You have missed the first class on the first day. That is not good, Colton."

"I promise, I will take—"

"No, it is too late. You are not ready for this. You cannot even respect the rules of Level One and report on time to take your first class. There is no way you can progress to Level Two. I'm not sure what we'll do with you."

"So does that mean I'll be sent to detention?"

Vincent paused. "No. That means we're sending you back. You will have to try another time."

"Back?"

"Yes. Back to Earth. To your last life."

Colton sat up straight and he gasped. "No, I don't want to go back there. I was just fired from my job, and my girlfriend dumped me, and I was miserable there. I like it better here. Can't I stay? I promise I'll be good and take all the classes you want. I just need—"

"No, Colton. Not this time. Maybe next time. We're sending you back now."

"What? Nooooo!"

Movement jostled Colton's body. Two paramedics peered at him as he lay on the gurney, a mask on his face and an IV in his arm. Sirens wailed as the ambulance raced down the street toward the hospital's emergency room.

One of the paramedics leaned closer, looking at his face. "Hey, he's awake now. Good. Vital signs are stable."

Colton raised his arm toward his face.

"No," the paramedic told him. "You just relax. Keep your oxygen mask on, you need it. We'll be at the hospital soon."

Colton tried to talk but no sound came out.

The paramedic patted him on the arm. "You were hit by a pickup truck. But you'll be okay. This is a good hospital. They'll take real good care of you. You just relax now. You're in good hands."

His eyes opened wide as he remembered—Heaven Level One! He was going to take classes. A familiar voice whispered in his ear. "Sorry, Colton, it's my fault. I'll be here to greet you again next time, and I promise I won't pull you away from your classes. Take care, buddy." A hazy image of his friend Julian appeared and then quickly dissipated.

"Here we are," the paramedic said as the ambulance parked in the back of the hospital. The back doors of the ambulance opened, and he was wheeled out and then quickly pushed through the doors into the emergency room as jolts of pain moved through his body.

~~~

DEFENDING THE RANCH

Clara Brady gazed out the window and took in the dirt, grass, and trees on the expansive ranch. She was grateful for the hired hands who helped them and took care of the cattle on a daily basis. She didn't know how they would manage without them.

She knew working the ranch was difficult, tedious, and constant work, but it was a source of pride for her family going back several generations, and she was honored and gratified to be part of it. Despite working so hard and the hot winds that were brutal this time of year in Texas, she wouldn't want to live anywhere else.

Glancing over at her pa, she saw the years of hard work and fatigue etched on his haggard features. It was a tough life, but she knew he was fiercely determined to keep going and protect his land, no matter the cost.

Feeling her gaze on him as he sat in his favorite old chair, her father glanced at her. Then he sat up straighter, coughed, and looked around.

"Pa, are you okay? Has that Morgan clan been coming onto our land again? I want to help you fight them off. I know I can help."

Logan shook his head. "Nah, ain't nothin' you can do. You just keep makin' those suppers that I like. That's enough."

Clara sighed and tried again. "I want to help defend our land. The Morgans have no right to it, and I'm tired of them trying. I know it gets hard for you, and you're not getting any younger. You could use my help."

Logan watched her for a few moments, then spoke, a hard edge to his voice. "They can't do nothin'. It's ours. And that Jed Morgan is pushing things too far. He has no right to our land, and he knows it. He tried to steal the Callahan's ranch down in the east valley last year, but they fought him off. Now he's coming here, thinkin' he can steal ours." He coughed again and cleared his throat. "I'll fight him off myself if I have to."

"Pa, I can help. I know how to shoot a gun."

He shook his head. "Now you listen to me, Clara. You leave that to the menfolk, and you stay out of harm's way. You shouldn't be shootin' no guns, ya hear me?"

She clenched her fists as anger burned inside. "Yes, Pa." She was proud of her ability to shoot a gun, and she knew she was getting better at it. She certainly didn't want to kill anyone, but she would if she had to. She would defend her home. Her boyfriend, Boone, had taught her how to shoot, and she was getting used to the feel of a gun and how to aim. In fact, she was getting pretty good at it, and each day she improved. She just needed a little more target practice. There was no reason in the world a girl couldn't shoot and help her pa.

She knew she should keep her mouth shut, but she couldn't. "Pa, I know you're having a hard time fighting them off by yourself. The Morgan clan keeps trying, and it's not ending. I'm worried about you, and I know I can help."

Her father's voice was cold. "No girl of mine is goin' to be shootin' no guns. And that's final. When my pa died, I inherited full rights to the deed to this land, and the boundaries are clear. If there's any fightin', it's gonna be us men doin' it. I don' wanna hear any more talk about this."

She bit down an angry response and gazed out the window again. A dark speck became visible at the far edge of their ranch, a growing dust cloud surrounding the speck as it drew closer. She stood up straighter. Was that Jed Morgan again? No, it was from the wrong direction. Maybe it was Boone.

"Pa, I think Boone is comin'." She couldn't stop the smile forming on her face.

Logan leaned forward in his chair. "And you stay away from Boone. He's not a good man. I've heard stories about him drinkin' and messin' around with the wrong kind of people. Mark my words, he's no good fer you. You deserve better than that."

Clara glared at her father. "Pa, I love Boone. And that's not gonna change." She stomped to the front door. After one more angry glare at her father, she went out onto the front porch and shut the door to wait for Boone. A hot, dry wind stirred up the dust and blew her hair across her face. Her father would never understand what Boone meant to her, and she would never let Boone go. He made her feel special like no one else ever did.

Her excitement grew as she watched Boone's imposing figure riding his horse, and then she heard the hoof beats as he got closer. She shuffled from foot to foot as her elation increased.

After Boone arrived and dismounted, Clara ran into his arms. "Hey there, handsome."

Boone kissed the top of her head. "Hey there yourself, Clara. Yer lookin' right pretty today." His deep green eyes gazed into hers and she felt herself melt.

"Thank you, Boone." She smiled at him. "It's so good to see you." She kissed him and then pulled back. "Hey, I need more target practice. I want to get better at shootin' a gun."

"Has that Morgan clan been botherin' you again?"

She nodded. "Yes. And I want to help defend our land."

Boone let out a long, slow breath. "I want to keep you safe, baby, but I agree. You should know how to defend yourself if you need to. C'mon, let's do some target practice. Then we can cuddle and have us a good time."

Clara giggled, feeling passion for him build. "Sounds good to me, handsome."

***

One month later, Clara washed the last of the lunch dishes and was beginning to dry them when a loud noise and shouting got her attention. She quickly dried her hands and looked out the window. Her pa was out there, his rifle in his hands. Scanning the area a short distance away, she could make out Jed Morgan at the top of the hill. Two other men were with him, probably his sons, and they were armed.

She snuck into her room, got her gun, and quietly ran out into the field at the side of the house, hiding behind a large tree.

"Hey Logan," Jed Morgan yelled to her pa. "I'm here to claim the land that is rightfully mine."

Logan raised his rifle. "This here is my land, and you know it. Get off my land before you get hurt. You are trespassin' and you are not welcome."

Jed laughed. "You won't shoot me. Besides, you're too old to even shoot straight. I'm hereby claimin' this land, and there's nothin' you can do about it."

124

Logan took aim. "Leave now, Jed. This is yer last warning."

"Before what? What ya gonna do, old man? Yer not gonna shoot me."

Logan pulled the trigger and a bullet whizzed close to Jed but missed him.

Jed glared at Logan, a combination of anger and shock on his face as his hand twitched on the handle of his gun. One of the other two men immediately raised his gun and fired.

Logan yelped and fell.

Fear and determination gripping her, Clara gasped and took out her gun. Carefully, she stood the way Boone had taught her, feet apart. Both hands holding the gun, she aimed carefully at the man who just shot her pa, held her breath, and slowly pulled the trigger. The recoil was strong, but she was prepared. The bullet hit its mark, and the man yelped, staggered, and went down. A combination of shock, relief, and pride flooded her.

Jed and the other man still standing looked for the shooter but did not see her. They ran to the man who had fallen, then their enraged gazes again searched the area.

Jed walked closer, his voice fierce. "You jes' killed my oldest son. You will die for that." He peered at Logan, still on the ground, then shifted his gaze and finally saw Clara holding a gun. "You!" he shouted at her, rage filling his voice. "No girl is gonna shoot my son. You've just sealed your own death warrant, you little bitch."

Jed raised his gun and aimed it at Clara as she took a shaky step back. Fear gripped her. Maybe her pa was right. Maybe she shouldn't have tried to help. Now he might lose his only daughter. Her legs grew weak.

A shot rang out.

Clara gasped and closed her eyes, expecting to feel pain. Nothing. Did he miss?

She opened her eyes and looked at Jed and saw a shocked look on his face as a red circle of blood grew larger on his shirt in the middle of his chest. His legs buckled and he fell to the ground.

Rustling near her made her jump with fright.

"It's okay, it's me," Boone said as he joined her. "I couldn't let him hurt you."

Clara stared at him. "You shot him?"

"You're damn right I did, and I'd do it again."

"Hey!" the remaining man from the Morgan clan shouted. "You killed him! You shot my pa and my brother! You killed them both!" He let out a wail of grief and anger before turning and running off.

Clara turned back to her boyfriend. "I didn't know you were here."

Boone ran his fingers through her hair. "I jes' got here and saw what was happenin'. I needed to protect you and yer pa."

"My pa!" she moaned, as she ran to where he was lying on the ground.

Logan writhed on the dirt, moaning, holding his bleeding leg. "He shot me," he said between breaths.

"You're alive," Clara said. "We'll get the doc here to fix you up."

"What about Jed ..."

Boone stepped forward. "Jed is dead, sir. He won't be botherin' you none after this."

Logan blinked. "Dead? Are ya sure?"

"Yes, sir. Yer daughter here shot and killed the man who shot you. Then I shot and killed Jed as he was aimin' at your daughter to seek revenge. They both are dead now."

Logan's eyes grew large. "Clara, you ..."

"Yes, Pa. I did. I shot him dead. Tol' you I could help."

Boone nodded. "She is a good shot, Mr. Brady. She done you proud."

"Thank you, Boone, thank you both." Logan struggled to sit up. "Now can you help me get back in the house?"

***

Doc Williams closed his black bag and looked at Clara and Boone. "Yer pa will be fine now. He jes' needs to rest that leg and let it heal." He looked back at Logan. "Logan Brady, now don't overdo it, you need rest so you can heal properly, ya hear me?"

"Okay, Doc, thank you," Logan said, watching the doctor collect his things and walk to the door.

Doc Williams paused at the door. "Call me if it gets worse, okay?"

Clara smiled. "Yes, we will. Thank you, Dr. Williams."

"My pleasure, ma'am. You take care of him. He's a good man, and he should heal up jes' fine now." He gave a warm smile, tipped his hat, and then left.

Clara returned to the side of her father's bed. "How are ya feelin', Pa? Do you need anythin'?"

Logan shifted his position. "Well now, I wouldn't mind a big bowl of that stew you were makin'. It sure smells good."

She laughed. "Sure, Pa, I'll get you some. And I'm glad you'll be okay."

"Hell, I'm jes' glad that Morgan ain't gettin' my land."

Clara looked defiantly at her father. "I tol' you I could shoot a gun, Pa."

"Yep, you sure did. And I thank you. And hopefully, you won't need to do that again."

Boone cleared his throat. "Mr. Brady, speaking of that, I wanted to let you know I went to the County zoning office and got a proper, certified, signed copy of the exact boundaries of your land, so no one can take it from you. It's legally yours. I have it here for you." He held up a white envelope. "And besides, with my inheritance, I jes' bought the ranch bordering yours on the west side, so I can help protect yer land. And yer beautiful daughter won't be far away once she's livin' there."

Logan squinted his eyes. "What? What do you mean?"

"Yes sir, Mr. Brady. I am askin' you fer yer permission an' blessin' to marry yer beautiful daughter Clara here, and I will do my best to always make her happy."

Logan smiled. "Well now, seein' as you helped save my life, my daughter's life, and my land, I can't refuse that. I hereby give you my blessin', son. And welcome to the family."

Clara turned to Boone, her eyes wide. "Are you askin' me to marry you?"

"I sure am, baby." He removed his hat and got down on one knee. "My sweet Clara, would you make me the happiest man in the world and be my wife?"

Clara laughed and clapped her hands to her chest. "Yes, yes, yes!" She threw herself into Boone's arms as he stood up, and buried her face in his chest as he held her tightly.

Logan cleared his throat. "When you two lovebirds are done here, can I get that bowl of stew?"

Clara giggled. "Comin' right up, Pa."

~~~

PEACE FOR HUMANITY

L iam stood at the peak of the mountain, gazing out over the view before him. For once, he was speechless. A sea of billowy clouds spread out below him in all directions. There were no sounds. There were no words. There was just complete, powerful peace.

He knew that down on the surface of the planet wars were being fought. Violent, bloody, horrible wars, filled with pain, destruction, and death. He ached deep into his soul. There was too much anger, hatred, and fighting down there. It had to end. It couldn't go on like this.

He pushed those thoughts aside. Liam had come up here, as he often did, to get a much needed break from the war. It was only a one-hour break, but it was desperately needed. This place was crucial for him to maintain his sanity.

For now, he allowed the serenity before him to settle in his body. He felt a deep peace wash through him, and that anchored him and gave him strength, as he took in the scene that surrounded him.

On this mountain, surrounded by clouds and snowy vistas, he touched the incredible expanse of infinite wonder. The beauty and overwhelming grandeur filled him, and he felt his muscles relax and the tension in his body soften.

But time was running out. His eyes burned with tears. Liam needed to lead his troops into battle one last time. One last desperate attempt to hold onto their freedom and their basic human rights. It was vital. It was life or death.

This needed to be the last war, the final battle, if humanity were to survive.

He took a deep breath, and his eyes took in the exquisite awe-inspiring magnificence before him. The incredible beauty and serenity of this place was not lost on him. This was what he needed, and what mankind needed, to survive. It was what made it all worthwhile. It was what they were living for and fighting for.

It was what too many people were dying for.

It was time to return to the world below. The planet and all of humanity were worth saving.

Please, God, he thought, *let this be the last war. Please.*

~~~

THE ASSIGNMENT

G reg looked at me, his clear blue eyes intense. "Laura, did you see our new assignment?"

"Yes," I answered, drumming my fingers on the table. Excitement ran through me as I anticipated the new job we were assigned. Greg was good at what he did. We both were. Working together for years as special agents, we grew close, but his intensity always unnerved me a bit. "We need to take down a bad guy. Interesting case."

"Fernando Rau," Greg clarified. "Definitely a bad guy." He glanced at his mug and sipped his coffee.

I nodded. I had seen the orders come through and I looked forward to it, even though a hint of anxiety crept in. "Take down? Or bring in?" I raised my eyebrows. I had no problem with either. I just wanted to be clear.

Greg put his mug down and looked at me. "Laura, I don't think this guy will give us a choice. He's a bad guy through and through, all the way to the bone. I really doubt that he will come with us peacefully."

I had to agree with him. "You're right. This one is dangerous. I remember reading the background information on him. He's killed before, many times. And with no reason." This guy made me a bit nervous. No matter how good we were at our job, some people were a wild card and could make things difficult and treacherous.

133

Greg nodded. "We'll meet him at the cabin—the one up in the woods by Bradford Fields. Fernando will be led to think there is a job for him there. At least that's the setup." His clear blue eyes bored into mine. I had no idea why the intensity in his eyes affected me so strongly. I blinked and looked away.

Adrenaline surged through my body. This was an important assignment, and I really wanted to get this guy. "I know the cabin. Just tell me when." I looked forward to taking this guy down. I knew a lot about him. He was unstable at best, and it was risky dealing with him.

***

I parked my car among the trees where it would be well hidden and walked a short distance through the woods to the cabin. I arrived thirty minutes early. The place was silent and looked deserted. A shiver ran through me. Did I have the date right? I double-checked the date and time in my head and then studied the area.

Greg said he would meet me here, but where was he? Something didn't feel right, and I remained alert. I waited a while, hidden in the trees. I checked my watch again—it was 4:00 p.m., exactly when he said he'd be here. Was he already here?

Greg was always punctual. Either he had gotten held up and was running late, or he was already stealthily hidden somewhere. I hoped for the latter. We had agreed to arrive separately and be discreet. We put our lives in each other's hands on a daily basis, and I trusted him with every fiber of my being. I needed to trust that he was already here.

A part of me realized I was also beginning to care for him more than I wanted to admit. But I would deal with that another time. For now, I needed to focus on taking down Fernando. And I needed to find this guy before he discovered me.

I observed the entire area, my eyes scouring every inch of the place. I didn't see any sign of him. On alert, my senses heightened, I held back for a while and carefully looked around, watchful and vigilant. There was potential danger everywhere, and especially now. Fernando was dangerous and unpredictable, and he could be hiding anywhere.

I surveyed the area for a few more minutes. No sign of anyone. Maybe he didn't show. Maybe he sensed something was wrong and he wasn't coming. Or maybe he was turning the tables on us and he was setting us up.

A chill ran up my spine. I slowly edged out of the trees and approached the dark cabin. After stopping and listening for any sounds, I warily started walking around the structure, peering in the windows.

As I rounded the far end of the cabin, I heard the click of a weapon.

A lump formed in my throat and I slowly turned toward the sound of the weapon. Fernando stood there, dressed in black, a black cap on his head, his face weathered. Dark scruff covered his chin, and a gun was held firmly in his hand. He meant business. He sneered. "Looking for me?"

Where was Greg? I desperately hoped he was here. I had to buy time. "I just want to talk, that's all."

Fernando spat on the ground. "No talking. You are the obstacle standing between me and my freedom. I know you want to take me down. I can't let that happen."

"No, you got it wrong. That's not what's happening here."

"Sure it is, little lady." His face contorted with rage. "You set me up, didn't you?"

"No, it's not like that." I needed to keep him talking. "Where will you go after this?"

He made a low guttural sound. "I'm getting far away from here. But it's none of your business where I will go. You won't be here anymore, anyway."

My nerves ramped up and I felt jittery, but I stayed calm on the outside. "I thought we could make a deal."

He furrowed his brows. "No deals. Enough talk. I don't trust you." His lips contorted in an evil taunt.

I stood still. I did not want to push him into doing anything risky. He was too far away for me to rush him and try to overtake him—he would shoot me before I reached him. I tried to think of possible things I could say that would deescalate things. I did not want to die there. "I just wanted to ..."

"Enough." Fernando's hand came up, the weapon aimed at me. I stopped talking. This was it. It could all end within seconds.

The sound of a shot pierced the air and I gasped, bracing for the impact.

Fernando's eyes opened wide in shock and the gun discharged as it fell from his hand, the bullet going wide into the trees. He slumped to the ground, a pool of red spreading out underneath him.

Greg stepped out from behind a tree and smiled. "Got you covered, babe." He moved to the body and kicked the gun away. Then he lightly kicked the body with his boot, but it was clear Fernando was dead.

I let out a big sigh of relief. I was not shot, Fernando was dead, and it was so good to see Greg. "Where were you?"

He grinned. "I was here but I could not give away where I was." Greg's eyes shone with intensity. "But I would never let anything happen to you."

"I trust you with my life, Greg. I always do."

His face lit up with a smile. "And I trust you with mine." He gestured to the body lying on the ground. "We need to take care of this and finish it."

I surveyed Fernando's body and nodded. "We need to get rid of it somewhere."

"For now, let's move it away from the cabin. Get it out of sight and clean up the area. We can't leave it here. Then we'll think about what to do with it."

"And we need to find that one bullet that he fired."

"I think I know where it went. We'll find it."

I looked into Greg's intense eyes and studied him for a few moments. "Okay, what's up?" I shook my head. After all this time working together, I could tell when he was holding something back. "There's something else going on here. What are you not telling me? Talk to me."

He chuckled. "This meeting had two purposes. One was getting the bad guy."

I glanced at Fernando's lifeless body lying a few feet away. "Done. And the other?"

Greg moved close to me and leaned in. "This." He took my face in his warm hands and placed a soft kiss on my lips. A tingle raced through me all the way to my toes.

I kissed him back, pressing into his soft lips, and a rush of heat flooded me. After all these years working so closely side by side, I ached for him. I wanted more. "Greg ..." I whispered.

He looked into my eyes, his gaze intense. "Laura, I'm not sure how to tell you this, and I know it breaks all the rules ... but I think I have fallen in love with you."

I smiled and felt my face flush. "I have fallen in love with you, too." My voice was soft.

He laughed and drew me into a tight hug, holding me against him for a few minutes. Then he pulled back and gazed into my eyes. "Let's take care of our friend here, and then let's go someplace more private and discuss this."

My whole body tingled. This would definitely be my favorite assignment.

~~~

GIFT OF LIFE

B rooke woke up to the sound of machines beeping, a sound that for some reason was soothing. *She was still alive!*

Her chest ached. But she had been reassured that was normal for just two days after her heart transplant. It had been agonizing waiting for an appropriate donor, and she was excited when one finally became available. It was her only chance at life.

For two weeks she remained in the hospital, hooked up to tubes, drains, IVs, and monitors. She felt weak and exhausted, and recovery was slow but steady. After following all the nurses' instructions and doing all the exercises given to her by physical therapy, it was finally time to go home. Although a bit nervous about leaving the safety of the hospital, she couldn't wait to go back to her own home. And with her husband working from home, it was reassuring to know she would have him there to help her.

The first month home was a vague fog of naps, exhaustion, a few exercises, walking, and a lot of gratitude. Then finally, she began to have more energy and feel better.

"Honey?" Brooke looked at her husband. "I was thinking about this whole experience. I am so grateful to have this new heart—I'm not sure how much longer I would have survived without it. This has really given me a new life."

Kyle smiled back at her. "It was a long time waiting for it. And I'm so glad you're still here with me. I was not ready to lose you."

She nodded and paused, collecting her thoughts. "I'm so glad to still be here. I didn't know if I would get one in time." She sighed. "This really changes everything. The young man who donated this heart truly gave me my life back. It's mind blowing."

"How are you feeling now?"

"Still weak, but so very happy and grateful." She thought for a few moments. "You know something? I'd really like to meet the family of the person who donated this heart. Is that possible?"

Kyle sat up straight. "That's a great idea. I'll call the hospital and see if it can be arranged."

"Good, thank you." She sipped some water. "Hey, you know what I'd really like?"

"What?"

"A violin."

Kyle's eyes opened wide with surprise. "What? You've never expressed any interest in the violin before. In fact, you've never played any instrument."

Brooke shrugged. "I know. But for some reason, I've been thinking about a violin lately. I don't know why, but it's been at the back of my mind for a few weeks now. I'd love to get one."

Kyle stared at her. "Are you serious?"

She nodded. "Yes, I really want one. It's all I can think about lately. Do you think we can find one?"

He hesitated. "Okay, I'll look for a used violin. I'm sure I can find one."

140

Two weeks later, he walked in the door. "Honey? I have a surprise for you."

Brooke looked up from where she sat at the kitchen table. "What is it?"

He placed a black case on the table in front of her. "Open it."

Fingers trembling, she opened the case and her eyes fell on a beautiful violin sitting in a red velvet liner inside the case. She sucked in a breath and her eyes opened wide. "It's beautiful." She slowly reached for the violin and reverently took it out of the case.

Kyle watched her as she inspected the instrument. "Do you like it?"

"I love it," she said, her voice subdued. "Thank you." Her eyes filled with love, she turned the violin in all directions and looked at every inch of it, running her fingers along the smooth surface. "This is magnificent," she whispered.

She shifted the violin and positioned it under her chin with her left hand just the way she had pictured it in her mind. Smiling, she reached for the bow and held it in her right hand. Slowly placing the bow over the strings, her hand shaking slightly, she drew the bow across the strings. A scratchy sound came out. She chuckled, held the bow more lightly, and tried again. This time, there was a sweet, pure tone. Her face lit up.

Kyle's mouth dropped open. "That actually sounded good. Where did this interest come from?"

She shrugged. "I don't know. I just felt a compelling need to do this." She glided the bow across the strings a few more times, playing a few more notes and eliciting melodic tones. Then she looked at the instrument. "I love this," she said softly. "I need to take lessons. I have to learn how to play."

After researching a few local teachers, she chose one and signed up for a few weeks of lessons. Feeling both nervous and excited, she went to her first lesson. Experienced and patient, the teacher covered all the basics, and Brooke took to it quickly, as though playing the violin was second nature. It filled her with an indescribably joy, and she spent hours practicing.

A few weeks later, she received a phone call from a voice she didn't recognize. "Hi, my name is Marcie. I'm not sure how to say this, but ..." The woman paused and took a deep breath before continuing. "I heard you wanted to meet the family of the donor heart you received."

Brooke sat up at attention. "Yes, yes, thank you."

"The heart you received is from my son. Would it be okay if I came to see you?"

"Yes, absolutely." A thrill went through her. "When can you come? I would love to meet you."

"How is Friday afternoon? I could be there around 2:00—is that good for you?"

"Yes, Friday is perfect. I look forward to meeting you."

***

Brooke made sure the house looked decent, and she baked cookies on Friday morning. She couldn't wait to meet the donor's family member. Part of her felt nervous. Would Marcie resent her for having her son's heart? Brooke at least wanted the chance to thank her and let her see that she had been given a new life because of what this woman's son had done with such an incredibly giving spirit.

In the afternoon, the doorbell rang, and a jolt of anxiety ran through her. She wasn't sure what to expect. Opening the door, she saw a middle-aged woman with light brown hair.

The woman smiled and held out her hand. "Hi, it's so nice to meet you." She hesitated. "My name is Marcie. My son, Will, was the heart donor."

Brooke shook her hand and then stepped back. "Come in, please. Let's sit down and talk." She led the way into the living room where a platter of her freshly baked cookies sat on the coffee table along with a pitcher of lemonade and two glasses. "Please make yourself comfortable and help yourself to some cookies."

Marcie gave a weak smile. "Thank you, you are so kind." She suddenly choked back a sob. "My son was ... killed ..." She cleared her throat and took a deep breath before she could continue. "He was killed in a car accident. He was only twenty-three years old. You have his heart." Tears filled her eyes and she quickly looked away and then back at Brooke.

Brooke bit her lower lip. "I'm so sorry for your loss. But from the depths of my soul, I thank you for the gift he gave me. I appreciate it more than you know. You raised a wonderful son, and he gave me my life back." She looked into Marcie's eyes. "Would you like to hear his heart beating?"

Marcie gasped and stared at Brooke, and then she nodded. "I'd love to." Brooke moved closer, and Marcie leaned in, placing her ear on Brooke's chest. With tears in her eyes, she listened to the sound of her son's heart beating in this woman's chest. She finally pulled back and gazed at Brooke. "That's the most beautiful thing I've heard. Thank you for that."

"Thank you," Brooke responded. "I wouldn't be here today if not for the wonderful gift that your son gave me. His heart beats on in me."

Marcie nodded, tears spilling down her cheeks. "This makes me so happy."

Brooke sat back. "Please tell me about your son."

Marcie smiled. "Will was the kindest person I've ever known. He would help anyone, and he wanted to make everyone happy." She thought for a few moments. "And he was a professional musician."

Brooke's eyes opened wide. "He was?"

"Oh yes, he played the violin in concerts and at various charitable events. He was really good. The violin meant so much to him. The music he played was straight from the heavens. You could hear the music crying and feel the loving touch of angels. It deeply touched my soul when he played."

Brooke stared at the woman. "This is too much of a coincidence."

Marcie looked confused. "What do you mean?"

Brooke glanced at her husband and then back at Marcie. "I've never played a musical instrument in my life. And then after receiving your son's heart, I had such a powerful urge to play the violin." She heard Marcie gasp. "I've taken some lessons. Would you like to hear?"

Marcie nodded, her face pale.

Kyle brought the violin to Brooke, and she positioned the instrument under her chin, reached for the bow, and slowly began to play. After she finished her song, she lowered the violin and looked at Will's mother.

Marcie's eyes were wide, her face wet with tears. "Amazing Grace. That was one of Will's favorite pieces."

Brooke took a deep breath. "Mine too. I can't play it enough."

Marcie stared at her. "But how is this possible? You say you've never played before?"

Brooke shook her head. "No, I've never played any instrument until I received Will's heart." She paused and held Marcie's gaze. "It's as though your son is using the violin to speak through me." She blinked a few times. "And I am deeply humbled and grateful to both of you."

Marcie broke down in sobs for a few minutes. After she collected herself, she looked up. "Will..." she whispered.

"Yes," Brooke said softly. "He lives on in me."

~~~

AFTERWORD

Thank you for reading this family and relationship short story collection, ***Beyond Connections.***

I sincerely hope you enjoyed these stories and that they opened up worlds of connection, stirred your emotions, and deeply touched your heart as you explored the beautiful, touching, and heart-gripping world of family and relationships!

If you enjoyed these stories, please check out my other short story collections:

- ***Beyond the Abyss*** – Science Fiction
- ***Beyond Terror*** – Thrillers, Horror, and Suspense
- ***Beyond Love*** – Love and Romance
- ***Beyond Connections*** – Family and Relationships

Thank you again for reading ***Beyond Connections!***

— *Lynn Miclea*
Author

ABOUT THE AUTHOR

LYNN MICLEA is a writer, author, editor, musician, Reiki master practitioner, and dog lover.

After retiring, Lynn further pursued her passion for writing, and she is now a successful author with many books published and more on the way.

She has written numerous short stories and published many books including thrillers, science fiction, paranormal, romance, mystery, memoirs, a grammar guide, self-help guided imagery, short story collections, and children's stories (fun animal stories about kindness, believing in yourself, and helping others).

She hopes that through her writing she can help empower others, stimulate people's imagination, and open new worlds as she entertains with powerful and heartfelt stories and helps educate people with her nonfiction books.

Originally from New York, Lynn currently lives in Southern California with her loving and supportive husband.

Please visit *www.lynnmiclea.com* for more information.

Books by Lynn Miclea

Fiction

New Contact

Transmutation

Journey Into Love

Ghostly Love

Guard Duty

Loving Guidance

The Diamond Murders

The Finger Murders

The Sticky-Note Murders

Short Story Collections

Beyond the Abyss – Science Fiction

Beyond Terror – Thrillers, Horror, and Suspense

Beyond Love – Love and Romance

Beyond Connections – Family and Relationships

Non-Fiction

Grammar Tips & Tools

Ruthie: A Family's Struggle with ALS

Mending a Heart: A Journey Through Open-Heart Surgery

Unleash Your Inner Joy – Volume 1: Peace

Unleash Your Inner Joy – Volume 2: Abundance

Unleash Your Inner Joy – Volume 3: Healing

Unleash Your Inner Joy – Volume 4: Spirituality

Children's Books

Penny Gains Confidence

Sammy and the Fire

Sammy Visits a Hospital

Sammy Meets Grandma

Sammy Goes to the Dog Park

Sammy Falls in Love

Sammy and the Earthquake

Sammy Goes On Vacation

Wish Fish: Book 1 – Discovering the Secret

Wish Fish: Book 2 – Endless Possibilities

ONE LAST THING...

Thank you for reading this collection of short stories, and I hope you loved them!

If you enjoyed this book, I'd be very grateful if you would post a short review on Amazon. Your support really makes a big difference and helps me immensely!

Simply click the "leave-a-review" link for this book on Amazon, and leave a short review. It would mean a lot to me!

Thank you so much for your support—it is very appreciated!

Thank You!

Printed in Great Britain
by Amazon

28459881R00089